DEMIGODS ACADEMY

DARKNESS RISING

BOOK
10

DEMIGODS ACADEMY

DARKNESS RISING

ELISA S. AMORE

KIERA LEGEND

CHAPTER ONE

NICOLE

*S*ighing, I sat back on the bench of the white, wooden gazebo, inhaling the cool night air.

It was always so fragrant there thanks to the lilacs and other flowers that grew nearby—they intertwined with the eight-foot hedges that made up the maze. Some of them bloomed only at night, so seeing them open up under the moon felt like I was in on their secret, something they shared only with me, which I loved.

After so many days of fighting and jumping back and forth through time, I felt at peace right then, in that place, even though I hadn't felt that for a long time.

Somehow, I was given another chance to have the life I'd always wanted, the one I deserved. Not everyone got a second chance, and I was grateful. I would do whatever I could to keep it.

Memories of the trip to London with Cade crossed my mind, of taking him to see Pinky—my only friend from my previous life. It had been amazing. Like we were just an ordinary couple in the first blush of new love, and I was showing him parts of me that he hadn't known yet. Aside from introducing him to my best friend, we saw all my favorite parts of London. Some of the places weren't what most tourists would consider visiting, but they had been an important part of how I'd lived.

That Cade had not just accepted them, but seemed to like them too, made me even more convinced that we were meant to be.

Honestly, I hadn't wanted it to end. I even considered escaping the academy and convincing Cade to stay in London with me, but I knew we had to return. We were Demigods now—well, I'd just become one, while Cade had been one for years.

However, I still didn't have any wings.

Secretly, I'd hope that when all my other powers

reached full fighting fashion, I'd suddenly grow another pair of wings—white ones like Cade and the others had. But that didn't happen, and my back remained just scarred, which hurt my soul more than I'd ever admit.

Hephaistos was still sore that I'd lost the metal ones he'd made for me during the fight with the Corpse King in Olympus. I figured we could make another pair together, but hadn't broached the subject with him yet. It was best to let him take his time to grumble over his lost creation first, then possibly warm up to the idea of me being underfoot in his forge.

A resigned sigh left my lungs and I closed my eyes, letting my head rest against one of the posts of the gazebo. A series of bright images suddenly flashed before my eyes, startling me, and making me knock the back of my head on the wooden panel. Stars spun in my vision, forcing me to blink.

Standing, I rubbed at the sore spot just as another set of images zipped by in my mind. Then one solid scene formed like a snapshot. It was so vivid and real, growing into something more, that I had to blink several times to test my eyesight. Testing to see if what I was seeing was actually there. Real, and not a vision or an illusion.

In front of me, in the middle of the gazebo,

appeared what looked like a door—frayed at the edges. An open door. It was nothing like the time portals I could open. This was something new. Something inside told me I should resist, but the temptation was too strong, so I peered into the velvety darkness...

Someone glanced back at me, bright eyes blinking out of the shadows. Instantly, I recognized the dark blue hair and the lightning scars along her cheek and neck.

"Melany?" I gasped.

She must've heard me say her name, because her brow furrowed, eyes squinting as she peered even harder through the thinned-out veil between my world and... I had no idea where she was.

Everyone said she was dead. I was sure of it, actually. Had I somehow opened a portal to the afterlife? I'd seen more terrifying things than any one person ever should have, and yet, something about a portal to the dead chilled me down to the marrow of my bones. That was saying something considering I'd just spent months going toe to toe with a zombie king and his zombie minions.

Tentatively, I moved closer to the doorway. I wasn't afraid of Melany or the apparition of her, but I definitely didn't want to be sucked into wherever she was. Melany's lips moved swiftly. She was obviously saying something to me, or maybe she was talking to someone else that I couldn't see. Either way, I couldn't hear her.

With a shake of my head, I tapped my ear. "I can't hear you!"

Melany moved closer to the door as well, and she cupped her hands around her mouth and spoke again. A vibration rumbled over me, through me, and I thought I could make out the word, "Who…" but that was it. She was probably asking who I was.

"I'm Nicole Walker. I'm at the academy…" When my curiosity overcame my nerves, I reached a hand toward the shimmering barrier, wondering if I could cross it. Then I snatched it away before the tip of my finger could touch it.

What if I had to die to cross? Wasn't that where she was, the afterlife?

Her head suddenly turned, and I thought that maybe someone entered the room where she was so she had turned to talk to a person—I was sure she was in a room, because the faint outline of several book-shelves was visible behind her. A shadow suddenly obscured her face, and she pulled away from the door before the portal vanished. It was as if it never even existed.

"Who were you talking to?"

When I swung around, I found Cassandra standing

near the first step into the gazebo, staring up at me. Her brow furrowed with worry.

At first, I hesitated to say anything, used to not having people all up in my business, but Cassandra and I had been through a shit storm together. I'd trust her with my life.

"I thought I saw… ah, that girl, Melany." I cleared my throat, which had suddenly gone dry and constricted, since I was a bit unsure that I hadn't just hallucinated the whole thing. Maybe I was going mad. People went mad with too much power, didn't they?

She rushed up the steps and swung around, looking into every corner of the gazebo. "Like here, in the gazebo?"

Shaking my head, I rubbed at my neck. "No, through a portal."

"One of your time portals?" Her brow furrowed tightly.

"This was different, I think. I'm pretty sure I wasn't looking back in time."

"What did you see, exactly?"

"Melany. I'm sure it was her…" My hand lifted to my hair. "Blue strands, scars…"

Cassandra nodded, wanting me to continue.

"She was in a room. A library, I think, but I'm sure she could see me too." The throbbing returned to my forehead, so I began to rub it. "At least I think she could. Then she was gone, and the portal vanished."

Moving over to one of the benches, Cassandra lowered herself onto it, a concerned pinch to her lips. "Do you think you were looking into another dimension? Into… the afterlife?"

"Maybe. I don't know." I sat down next to her, exhaustion catching up to me.

"Don't tell anyone in the academy about this," she cautioned, "especially not Lucian."

"I won't."

"Maybe you were just seeing things." She eyed me curiously. "You were complaining earlier about having bad dreams and getting flashes of images in your head. Could be just residual memories of seeing Melany before."

My fingertips massaged circles over my forehead again, harder this time. "Yeah, maybe."

Sighing, Cassandra's gaze scanned the area. "Where's Cade?"

"In his room." I stretched out my neck, giving it a good crank left and right. "I needed some 'me' time."

"You should be resting."

I eyed her carefully. "So should you."

"I needed some 'me' time as well. Everyone means well but…"

"Yup, that big ole but..." I chuckled. "Gets you every time."

"I'll go back, if you do," Cassandra offered, standing.

"Yeah, I guess."

She extended her hand to me, and I took it, letting her pull me to my feet. "I'll fly you back if you want?"

I shook my head. "No thanks. I've had my fill of being flown around, to be honest. I'd much rather use my own two feet and walk."

"Do you want company?" she asked wistfully.

"Nah, mate. I'm good."

"All right." Her lovely expanse of white-feathered wings unfurled, and I fully admitted to being jealous. Especially since I knew I'd never have the same. "I'll see you later."

"Yes, you will." My lips curved into a cheeky grin.

Returning the smile, she flapped her wings once and took to the air. My gaze followed her as she rose above the maze's tall hedges, then flew toward the looming dark spires of the academy. Then I was alone once more.

Cade would probably be hurt to hear it, but I liked my solitude. I'd been on my own for long enough to accept that I worked well by myself. However, I'd also learned in these past few weeks that I needed other people. Needed to let them in, needed to trust them. Cade in particular.

As I walked along the path, I thought about what I saw in the gazebo. Maybe Cassandra had been right and I was hallucinating, seeing things from my dreams, or from the infinite number of times I'd jumped back and forth through time.

That had to have messed up my head.

How could it not?

If it had truly been Melany though, or a version of Melany, then I wasn't sure how and why I'd been able to open a window into the afterlife, wherever or whenever that was. It was definitely strange seeing her, knowing bits and pieces of her story. She was a legend at the academy, and according to others, she was one in the mortal world as well. I heard they erected a statue of her in the square of her hometown, after she literally saved the town and all its people from death.

The ripples of her existence still flowed through both worlds and through the people she'd known.

A shiver ran down my body, so I pulled the edges of the coat I was wearing tighter as I rounded another corner, taking the straight path out of the maze. Or at least I hoped it was the right path, because sometimes the maze rearranged itself.

To be honest, the whole encounter in the gazebo

had shaken me. I was still a bit unstable from almost being erased from existence, and I wasn't completely sure that all my atoms had realigned themselves into my body properly. Everyone insisted that I was whole, that I was complete, and still the same Nicole, but some moments I questioned that truth. How could they truly know anyway, when I wasn't even sure?

And now this, seeing a rip in time and space, seeing someone who was supposed to be dead...

I shook my head. Nope, I wasn't going to address it. I was done. I was tired. I needed to rest, sleep, and eat for at least a week before I could function properly and deal with what I'd experienced.

As far as I was concerned, what happened in the gazebo didn't happen. Cassandra wasn't going to say anything to anyone, and neither was I.

When I walked out of the maze, I breathed a sigh of relief. I'd return to the academy, find Cade in his room, wrap my arms around him, and kiss him until my mind emptied of everything except for how his lips felt on mine. That sounded like the perfect plan. I just hoped I didn't mess it up during the amount of time it took me to walk from here to there.

CHAPTER TWO

NICOLE

*O*ver the next few days, I pushed the strange encounter I had with the Melany apparition out of my mind, trying to relax and settle into the mundane life at the academy.

It was odd not to be opening time portals and jumping through them, all in an effort to save the world and everyone in it, which was what I'd been doing since leaving London. I supposed anything would seem boring after that.

Surprisingly, I did manage to settle into a bit of a routine. I slept—sometimes in my bed, sometimes in Cade's, which usually wasn't all that relaxing but was absolutely more enjoyable. He was definitely a cuddler and crazy good with his hands.

Then I got up, went to the dining hall and ate. Eating in the hall was my favorite thing. Actually, eating in general was my favorite thing, my number one hobby. It was probably because I'd gone years without knowing where I was going to get my next meal, so having a literal smorgasbord of food at my fingertips was a dream. And you better believe I indulged at every opportunity.

Even if I hadn't been so obsessed with food, we Demigods needed a ton of fuel to support our turbocharged metabolisms, so I definitely wasn't the only one who haunted the dining hall during all hours of the day and night.

After getting my fill of spaghetti, cheesy lasagna, crispy fish tacos, chicken parmigiana, pepperoni pizza, juicy fruit salad, and rich chocolate cake, all washed down with my favourite indulgence of icy cold Pepsi, I'd meet Jasmine and Mia out on the east training field for some physical conditioning. Not that I wasn't strong, I was—I could run for miles, and I had battled the Corpse King and his undead minions with my fire power—but they insisted. Well, Jasmine mostly insisted that I could be stronger and faster with the right amount of fitness training.

Since I didn't have wings, not until I got a new set of forged metal ones, I needed to be quicker on my feet if I was going to evade an enemy. And once I returned to the academy, I quickly came to understand that there was always going to be another enemy.

The training was basically Jasmine, armed with a spear, chasing after me while I ran across the field as fast as I could. A couple of times, Tinker showed up and cheered me on from the sidelines with his joyful bleeps and bloops. If I wasn't fast enough, Jasmine would poke me in the back with the blunted tip of her spear. I'd been poked a few times now, that left small round bruises on my skin.

Just another day as a Demigod.

Cade got the task of rubbing healing salve on my back every night. Something he never complained about—and I actually figured he quite liked, because almost every time, we would end up rolling around on the bed, mine or his, kissing, muscles bunching under soft caresses.

Thankfully, during those few days, I didn't get painful flashes of images in my head, or opened any strange portals to who knew where to see people who were long gone. Maybe Cassandra had been right, and it was just an illusion brought on by continuous time jumps. Aside from that, my days were all rather dull and uneventful. Which wasn't necessarily bad. It wasn't like I was aching to go off running into another dangerous adventure, or at least, that's what I kept telling myself.

On the fourth day, while I was out on the field learning how to dodge Jasmine's lethal spear, Prometheus called me to his office. Well, I guess it wasn't really called so much as being escorted by a guard who showed up on the field, taking me to the great golden hall where Prometheus's private rooms were situated. I supposed it would've been stranger to have been summoned by an overhead speaker system like that in a human school. *"Nicole Walker, please report to Headmaster Prometheus's office."*

When I got there, he gestured for me to sit in one of the large leather chairs and offered me a beverage from a golden decanter. I was pretty sure it was wine, but I declined. I could never get used to the taste of wine, neither crisp white, dark, or rich red. If I chose to drink, it was usually something hard, like vodka or rum. Something that would make my mind fuzzy and relaxed, fast. There had been many nights in my past of drinking an entire bottle with my best friend Pinky.

"I'll take some water if you have it," I replied, settling into the oversized chair. Sweat was still dripping down my back from the workout Jasmine and Mia had given me.

"Of course." Picking up a clay jug, he poured the cool, clear liquid into a large goblet and handed it to me.

The water refreshingly swept down my throat, while I marveled at the idea that the cup I was drinking from was like over two thousand years old. So many things here were ancient, yet everyone treated them like nothing special. However, I looked at those pieces and always wondered about the hands they had passed through, or the stories they could tell. I supposed that was just my time genes musing about the past.

Prometheus sat in the opposite chair and regarded me, his wide, heavy brow wrinkled in concern. "So, how are you, Nicole?"

"I'm good." Part of me wondered why he was asking; I still found it hard to trust those with authority. Although Prometheus had come through for us by informing Chronos of the plan to unravel time and the Gods themselves—he did technically save my life—I was wary. When it involved the Gods and Titans, I wasn't sure I would ever not be cautious. Nothing they did was straightforward.

"You are settling back into the academy? Getting your training?"

I nodded. "Yup, Jasmine is a tyrant when it comes to that stuff."

Prometheus chuckled. "She's tough. I've seen her teach battle tactics to the new recruits. Ares would've been envious."

"Yeah, you should give her a raise." My throat was getting drier by the second, so I drank more water. He wanted something from me, I could sense it in every bone in my body.

"After you've gone through more training, it would be helpful to the academy if you joined the others to train the new recruits. You have many skills that would be an asset were they passed down."

Training recruits was not something I had in mind for myself, I didn't do well with people. I liked Lucian, Jasmine, Georgina, and the others, but despite all we'd been through together in a short while, I still didn't feel like part of the team. I was an outsider, and even though I knew they didn't mean to, they treated me like one.

Except for Cassandra. She was someone I could call a friend. I supposed that was what happened when you faced certain death together, and we had done that a few times. Facing down a T-Rex in real life Jurassic Park kind of made you life long buddies.

"I know you've been through a lot," Prometheus

added once he finished his wine, then got up to refill his cup. "You have suffered." He sat back down and met my gaze. "I know a lot about suffering. You and I are a lot alike in that regard."

It was true that Prometheus had suffered.

The students told stories about what he went through thanks to Zeus and the Gods. Because of his affection for mortals thousands and thousands of years ago, he stole fire from the Gods to give it to the humans so they could use it for warmth and to cook. For his unselfish act, Zeus ripped Prometheus away from his life and imprisoned him in Tartarus, along with all the other Titans.

The rumor was that while in prison, Prometheus's liver was eaten by crows. Yet, once it grew back, it would be eaten all over again in an endless loop. A weaker man would've gone mad, but Prometheus seemed to have kept his humanity and affection for mortal men and women even after what he endured.

"I was wondering…"

Oh, here it comes.

"…if you would be willing to do something for me. It's a big ask."

"That depends. What do you want? And what do I get in return?"

His bushy eyebrows shot up at that. He was probably not used to people pushing back on him. I imagined all his requests were immediately answered without question, but I wasn't one of those people. I was tired of being taken advantage of and used. The Corpse King had seen to that. Pushing me to jump through time again and again until I could barely stand, barely think.

"I know you have been through a lot, forced to jump through time by Lycaon. But I wanted to ask you to take me back in time, to see my wife before I was torn from her side and tossed into a hellscape for thousands of years." Placing his wine goblet onto the small, round table between our chairs, he set his gaze on me.

Shit. Didn't I feel like an asshole now?

"What do you want in return for this request?" he continued. "I will try and give you whatever you wish, but obviously, there are limits to what I can offer."

It wasn't hard to imagine that one of those limits would be allowing me to leave the academy with Cade, to go and live a normal life back in London. So, I pushed that thought out of my mind right away, deciding I wasn't even going to bother to mention it. What else did I want? What would make me happy, and my life here in the academy bearable?

"I want to work in the forge. I don't want to have to deal with new recruits. I just want to work with the metal and make stuff. Not weapons necessarily, but I could do that as well. I want to create cool things, like more robots. I couldn't ever duplicate Tinker, but maybe I could make him a companion."

With a chuckle, Prometheus nodded. "I'm unsure of what Hephaistos will think about this, but ultimately, he'll do what is best for the academy. And having you in the forge would be a good thing. Your affinities to fire and metal are an asset. I'm sure we can convince Hephaistos of that."

Ha! He had more faith in our negotiation skills than I did. Although, I had been able to get Hephaistos to help me make my wings. I supposed that if I promised him to literally stay out of this way, he might warm up to the idea. It would take a load of work off his shoulders. Plus, he was eons old, and I thought that maybe it was starting to catch up to him.

"I also don't want anyone to know that I'm taking you through time. It must be a secret. I don't want a lineup of people asking me for the same thing. I'm not British Airways."

"Agreed." He nodded firmly and reached over, offering me his hand, which I accepted. His hand was so huge that it swallowed mine to the wrist. We shook, sealing the deal. "You have no idea what this means to me, Nicole. I will forever be in your debt."

"You're welcome. I know a little something about having your life ripped away without your consent." I swallowed when a few flashes of me in a windowless room, tied to a chair, with Apollo literally squeezing my head as if he wanted to crush it like a melon played before my eyes. He entered my mind and tore it into a thousand pieces. Pieces I was still slowly collecting and putting back together. It was getting better, but I suspected I would never be completely whole again.

"I know you do." Kindness shone in his gaze as he let me go. "So, when can this happen?"

I jumped to my feet. "No time like the present."

His eyes widened in shock. "Now?"

"Yes, why not? I'm all fueled up and ready to fly." That way, I wouldn't have time to find an excuse not to do it, or remember how it felt to jump too many times.

We were just going through once. I could do it one more time for him. It wouldn't kill me. Not anymore.

CHAPTER THREE

NICOLE

"Is there anything I need to do?" Prometheus asked when I directed him to stand with me in the middle of his office. There was something unsettling about him asking me to explain something to him, the Titan who usually knew it all.

I gripped his hand tightly. "Think about your wife. Think about the place you want to go to see her. A house, or a street, or wherever. Picture it in your mind. See the colors, smell the aromas in the air, sense the place under your feet. Immerse yourself in the vision."

With a settling breath, I concentrated firmly on the air around us—stretching it out like taffy, making it as thin as possible for us to slip into and travel through it. I didn't know where we were going, so I had to rely on Prometheus's will to guide us. In the past, I had known where we were going to jump. I could picture it in my mind. There had been a few exceptions, of course. Like the first jump to the war between the Gods and the Titans, our trip to Paris in time to see Melany and Hades take on the giant Oceanus, and when I took Cassandra, the Corpse King, and myself, to the Jurassic Period.

All the other times I'd directed it, the location had come from me, and that was easier for me, taking up less of my energy. This time, it was going to come from Prometheus.

"I hope you're ready," I warned him. "The jump is startling, and I'm not one hundred percent sure I can get us to where you want to go."

"All I can ask is for you to try."

Nodding, I pulled my power close to me. "Okay, let's give it a go."

After closing my eyes, I tried to connect to Prometheus, in the same way I'd connected to Cassandra that first time she took me to see Chronos in her vision. I concentrated on him, on what he was thinking. Instantly, a rush of warmth and emotion swept through me, startling in its potency, but I guessed that was because he was a Titan.

The sensation filled me up like warm water being poured into a glass, bathing me, washing me clean. At first, I didn't really get what the feeling was, but when tears started to well in my eyes from an overabundance of pressure in my chest, I understood it. It was love. I blinked them away before they could spill over and track hot down my cheeks.

Prometheus's love for his wife was strong, and it was true.

Part of me hoped it would be enough of a connection to jump us in time to where and when she was located.

My focus increased, envisioning the white tunnel we'd jump through, constructing it around us in my mind. Then the surrounding air shimmered and vibrated, its molecules moving wildly along our skins. Prometheus's leathery hand tightened in mine—so much that he nearly crushed my bones, but I stopped myself from wincing—and then we were sucked through the thin veil of time and space.

Seconds later, we appeared in the middle of a dark, shadowy courtyard, dimly lit by a couple of torches stuck in the ground. Surrounding us on all sides stood a two-story house, built from bright white clay with a red shingled roof. Voices came from one of the rooms near the walled entrance.

"This is my home," Prometheus whispered in reverence. Longing exuded from him as he reached out a hand, the desire to touch it bright and clear.

The voices got louder, and I pulled him back into the shadows along the opposite wall. The next moment, two women appeared, dark yellow tunics that just reached past their knees covering their strong bodies, and their dark hair piled up onto their heads. Each carried a large clay bowl that reminded me of the cup Prometheus had served me water in a minute ago. Chatting amicably with each other, the women exited one of the rooms and went into another.

"Those are my two servants, Theodora and Agnes." Wonder captured him and he reached out again, but I grabbed his arm as I sensed he wanted to greet them.

"You can't interact with them. You don't know how it will affect the future."

He cast me a sidelong glance, and I realized that I couldn't stop him from doing anything he really wanted to do. Time to redirect.

"Where is your wife?" I asked, glancing toward the stairs that I assumed led up to another part of the house, the bedrooms, I thought.

"She is upstairs right now, bathing. I'm in the storeroom, taking inventory of our supplies. I am to be taken by Zeus and Ares this night for giving fire back to the people. She will never see me again, and won't know what happened to me."

Before I could respond to that, there was a commotion at the main door of the estate. A defiant shout echoed, followed by a flash of blinding light, a groan, and a thud. The door burst open and I caught sight of a man with a white beard and hair, wearing a white robe.

Knowing what was to come, Prometheus grabbed me and pulled me into the room behind us before we could be spotted. It was dark, so I didn't know what the space was, but it smelled of earth, dirt, and plants. It was both dry and rich, pleasant, so I assumed it must've been some kind of food storage area.

We stayed there as more shouts came from beyond, followed by screams and grunts of pain. Prometheus's muscles flinched with every noise, and suddenly his voice came from the courtyard—which was freaky, considering he was standing right beside me.

"You will never take me!" he commanded, *he* meaning the other Prometheus.

"You will come with me, old friend, or Ares will slice your wife's throat from ear to ear." Zeus's voice was like a rumble of thunder, dark and bold.

I would always remember that voice… It still gave me nightmares.

Ares's chuckle came soon after. Although the God of War had mellowed out after that, training young people for hundreds of years without killing anyone— as far as I knew—I suspected he hadn't really changed all that much. I'd heard the stories from Jasmine and the others, about the machinations of murder and betrayal he'd performed with Aphrodite in the shadowed hallways of the academy. As the God of War, he loved carnage. It was the essence of who he was.

A shiver rushed down my spine, and my stomach roiled in response. However much I wanted to race out there and stop what was going on, I knew I couldn't. Risking a glance at Prometheus, I saw that he, too, was fighting back the urge. His hands fisted at his sides, forced breaths coming in and out of his lungs as if it took everything he had not to act.

"I will come with you, but you must promise to spare my wife and the rest of my household."

There was a slight pause. "Agreed," Zeus finally acquiesced.

After a few minutes, silence spread through the courtyard.

"What do you plan on doing?" I asked Prometheus, unclear about why we'd come here for him to experience this horrible night all over again. Why would he want to witness this tragic and painful moment again?

We waited another few moments while Prometheus rested against one wall, his eyes closed, and I suspected he was trying to gather himself. Suddenly, a new voice echoed from the courtyard. A female one, and she was in so much distress that it made my throat tighten and my gut clench from hearing it in her shrill voice.

"What has happened?" she demanded. "Where has my husband gone?"

Other voices tried to console her—male and female —attempting to explain. Although, it sounded to me like no one really knew what had transpired. Were those who saw Zeus and Ares enter dead already, before Prometheus had struck the bargain with the all-powerful God? To the rest of the household, it prob-ably looked like he had just disappeared into thin air.

"Where is my husband?" she screamed.

The sound vibrated over my skin, making me both shiver and sick to my stomach. Prometheus's form sagged against the wall.

"The Gods took him, Mistress." The answer came from a young boy.

"Are you certain, Atticus? Did you see them?"

"I was hiding behind the wine barrel, but I saw an old man in white and a large man in armor. Lightning sparked from the old man's hand. It was Zeus, I'm sure."

"Maybe he will return, Mistress," a young woman suggested. Probably one of the servants I'd seen carrying the bowls. "Not all who go with the Gods perish."

"Let us take you to your rooms, where you can rest," said a different woman.

Sounds of shuffling and movement beyond the wall of the storeroom mixed in the air, then there was silence. The only thing I could hear was the bleat of several goats in a pen nearby, and Prometheus's ragged breathing.

My gaze focused on him. "What's your play here? Why did you want to come?" I whispered.

"I need to see her; I need to see Pyrrha."

"You can see her, but you can't interact with her. You understand that, right? You could alter history, and not necessarily in a good way. You don't know the ramifications of it. You could end up creating a new war."

"There must be a way I can end her suffering without affecting the future."

I considered all the options and just didn't have a definitive answer for him. Anything, any alteration to this timeline, might change the future. However, thinking about my studies on the Gods, and on

Prometheus in particular, nothing stood out to me as a red flag. He was basically locked up in Tartarus for thousands of years—his liver torn out on repeat. Maybe what he did here wouldn't create any ripples.

"Perhaps you could write her a short note. Just let her know you love her or something, and that you didn't purposely leave her."

For a moment, I thought he might refuse and fight me to go see her regardless—and frankly, there wouldn't have been anything I could've done to stop him, he was a huge man—but he gave me a curt nod. A few seconds later, he rummaged around the shelves and tables, finding a papyrus scroll and a piece of char-coal to write.

I kind of felt like a voyeur in this situation, and I supposed I was, technically, so I moved away from him to give him some privacy. It wasn't my intention to intrude on the traumatic, emotional pain he was obvi-ously experiencing—so strong that I could almost feel it as my own. While he wrote his note, I slowly opened the door and peered out into the dark courtyard.

It was still vacant, which was good for us. We really didn't need someone to see us sneaking around the house. I knew better than anyone how even the smallest of actions, one extra shoe print in the mud, could change the future in unimaginable ways. The treads of a modern shoe caught in the dust of the past sent ripples that echoed for centuries.

"I'm done."

Turning, I found Prometheus rolling up the small scroll. "Okay, we can leave it maybe with a servant or…"

Taking me by surprise, especially since he moved so quickly, he went out the door of the dim, sheltered storeroom and into the sunny courtyard. The hot, humid air outside carried the bright scent of fresh lemon and the acrid aroma of eucalyptus.

"What are you doing? We already discussed this, mate." I had to rush to catch up to him.

"I need to see her. I won't talk to her, but I just need to lay my eyes upon her one last time." There was something in his voice, a note that made a fissure open in my heart, and if it hurt me, I couldn't even begin to fathom how he was feeling.

"What if someone sees you? You're supposed to be taken by the Gods, remember? It will really confuse the issue at hand."

There was nothing I could do to stop him; my powers were nothing against his. He wasn't listening to me either, no surprise there, and was already climbing the steps hewn roughly from stone—worn smooth from countless feet that climbed up to the second floor, where I assumed were the bedrooms. I might not be able to stop him, but I definitely couldn't let him go alone, just in case I needed to jump us out of there in a flash. Sighing, I followed him to the last room.

Once there, he slowly opened the heavy iron and wood door and peered into the space. Thankfully, it was dark inside, so we wouldn't be immediately spotted. Yet, if someone was really staring into the shadows, they would see a young woman wearing sweat pants and a t-shirt—aka, they would see "modern me", standing beside a giant of a man in white robes.

"Just leave the note on the bed," I whispered to him.

Thankfully, Prometheus did as I instructed, but then he stepped out of my reach. He seemed drawn like a magnet, tugged along like he was driven by a force he was powerless to resist. Extending his hand, he gently touched the sleeping woman's face, and despite my best intentions, I leaned closer too. I was curious. So that was his wife.

Her face was pleasant enough, her olive skin clear and smooth with full lips and thick, long hair, but she was no great beauty. That surprised me, because a Titan could have anyone he wanted, couldn't he? Still, as I tried to look at her through his eyes, I could see that there was something lovely about her, even with her eyes closed.

A murmur escaped his wife in her sleep, and she shifted beneath a coarsely woven sheet. It seemed that she still slumbered, but then she rolled toward him. If she woke and saw him, we'd be in trouble.

Immediately, I grabbed his arm, or tried to, because his arm was almost the size of my leg. "Let's go."

I thought for sure he was going to fight me on it, but he got to his feet and followed me out of the room without protest. The smell of cool dust and stone hung in the short corridor, and suddenly I swore I saw the shadows undulate before we reached the stairs. Out of thin air, a ball of fire sparked in someone's hand, its orange glow illuminating a chiseled, pale face.

"Prometheus? Aren't you supposed to be in Tartarus by now?"

Oh shit. I knew that voice and face, and I did not want to see them here and now, or anywhere, really.

Hades.

CHAPTER FOUR

NICOLE

"$\mathcal{H}$ades? What are you doing here?" Prometheus asked, a hint of wariness shading his hushed words.

"I've come to make sure your wife is safe, because you're supposed to be shackled in prison, and I do not trust my brother, no matter what he says."

I wasn't sure if Prometheus believed him, as his hands curled into fists, the slightest of sneers curling his lips.

Hades's gaze was suddenly on me. He looked me up and down, probably taking in the clothing I was wearing, which didn't fit the era at all. His brow furrowed. "You look vaguely familiar. Have we met before?"

I shook my head briskly, a tremor passing through me. "Nah, mate. I just have one of those faces, I think."

"No, you most certainly do not." The way he looked at me was piercing, his eerie eyes seeming to see right through to my core.

"Don't tell anyone you saw him here," I said to Hades sharply, knowing that I needed to do something to take charge of the situation. He was clearly startled to be on the receiving end of an order, especially from some strange, nothing girl he didn't know, but I ignored it. Then I grabbed Prometheus's hand. "We need to leave. Now."

Hades's mouth opened, probably respond with some kind of quick retort, or more likely, an order to tell him exactly who I was. Before he could, however, I focused on thinning the air, stretching it out like warm honey, and jumping us back to the academy.

Panicking, I didn't have time to consider the repercussions of Hades seeing us disappear. Would he able to tell from the thinning of the air around us that we were actually moving through time, jumping from one era to another? I really, really hoped he'd shake it off, maybe chalk it up to too much wine, then forget about it over the next three thousand years. Though, I'd never find out, as he was dead and gone in my timeline, so I wouldn't be able to ask about that time he saw us in Prometheus's house.

Then we were sucked into the white void, the molecules of the air vibrating against my skin in a way that was familiar to me by now. The portal spit us out back in Prometheus's office, as if we'd never left, only a second of time passed.

The Titan stumbled sideways a little, and he had to grab his desk not to completely fall. I, on the other hand, was as steady as a horse—since I'd done this for what felt like a million times.

"Did you just do a jump?"

My head whipped up to see Cade with Lucian and Demeter, standing just inside the office's entrance. They must've just arrived, or Prometheus and I had been gone more than a second, otherwise I would've seen them darkening the doorway right before we jumped.

"Yes," Prometheus confirmed. His voice was rough, and I knew he was still struggling with the aftermath of having seen his wife for the first time in thousands of years. He cleared his throat, pulling an invisible mask over his face as he did. "Academy business."

Not wanting to out him, I didn't flinch at the lie, but by the way Cade's eyes narrowed at me, I sensed he knew that wasn't true. I'd probably tell him later what happened and wouldn't even feel bad about it, because I knew I could trust him.

Yet, what I really wanted to know now was if seeing Hades had somehow altered anything in this timeline.

"Is Hades here?" I asked cautiously, testing their reaction to my words.

Everyone frowned, especially Lucian. He took a step toward me, his stare intent on my face. "Why are you asking?"

"Is he? I need to know."

"No, he's not here. He's gone." Lucian licked his lips, as if something in his mouth tasted wrong.

Breathing a sigh of relief and glanced at Prometheus.

Cade came to my side. "What happened?"

"I'll tell you later," I responded quietly.

Prometheus gathered himself, straightening his robe, and set his gaze on Demeter. "Why are you in my office? You don't normally come up here unless…"

"Something's going on in the mortal realm," Demeter explained.

Prometheus ventured over to the drinks table and poured himself a very large goblet of wine. I didn't blame him after our upsetting trip. If I were more of a drinker, I'd be a few shots in already, feeling the buzz in my head. "Tell me."

"There is word that one of the temples in Pecunia has been vandalized," Demeter explained.

"Word from where?" Prometheus's heavy brow furrowed.

Lucian glanced at Demeter and gave her a knowing look. With a roll of her eyes, she slid out a cell phone from a pocket in her billowy green tunic, handing it to the Titan. "It's all over the news."

The phone was tiny in Prometheus's hand as he looked down at it, then shook it. "How does it work?"

At first, I thought he was joking, but then I saw the perplexed arch to his brow. Taking it from him, I opened an app, and showed him the first newsclip. It was a video of a reporter standing in front of one of the larger temples, one that looked like Zeus's, while she gestured to the graffiti and damage done to the usually white marble.

I wasn't a stranger to graffiti and vandalism, but even the level of damage on that one was surprising to me. Temples weren't usually vandalized. Despite the type security some had, kids and graffiti taggers just didn't resort to that type of criminal act. Not to a house of worship.

"Has this ever happened before here, in his

district?" Prometheus asked Demeter, since he'd only been Headmaster at the academy for the past three years.

She shook her head, her clunky wire earrings getting tangled in her wild curly hair. "Nope. We've experienced total destruction by a Titan, but not from mortal hands. This is something new."

"Okay. Lucian, take a team to Pecunia and check it out. Talk to the locals and to law enforcement and see what you can find out. Ask if they have any ideas on who did this and why."

"I'll let you know what we discover." Giving Prometheus a curt nod, Lucian turned to leave.

Demeter wandered over to the drinks table. "Got any more of that wine?"

Without answering, Prometheus poured her a goblet.

Before Cade and I could leave, the Titan nodded to me. "Thank you, Nicole."

Offering him a tight small smile, I nodded back, and then left with Cade. His arms instantly wrapped around me, then he flew me back down to the main level.

"I'd wondered what happened to you," Cade admitted when we landed. "I went looking for you on the training field, but Jasmine said you were summoned to see Prometheus."

"He wanted a favor."

"Judging by the looks on your faces when you returned, that favor wasn't so easy."

I shook my head. "No, it wasn't. Not as tough as going to the ends of time and space, but equally as draining."

Cade took my hand in his and gave it a reassuring squeeze just as Lucian whirled to face us.

"Why did you ask me about Hades?"

Part of me thought I owed him an explanation. It probably wasn't so easy for him to talk about the God who stole his girl. "While jumping with Prometheus we ran into him. I needed to make sure that seeing him and talking to him didn't alter the future."

"It didn't."

"Well, technically, you wouldn't know that. If the time-line changed at all, your reality would've changed with it, so you'd only know the truth as you experienced it."

He shook his head. "Sounds way too complicated."

"It is."

"Are you two coming to Pecunia with the crew?"

With a shrug, I glanced at Cade. "Sure, why not? Beats sitting around here. I'm bored."

. . .

THE CREW CONSISTED OF LUCIAN, Jasmine, Georgina, Ren, Cade and I because Cassandra stayed behind to help Chiron go through his healing potions, tinctures, and supplies. After our nearly fatal trip through time, she wanted to get better at healing even though she was pretty good already, and had helped save my life. Jasmine's girlfriend, Mia, also remained, to take over the training of the new recruits at the stables.

Since the attack by the undead and the Corpse King, she'd been helping rebuild it, as well as train the new fire horses and griffins.

Ready for our mission, we all gathered together in a cave just beyond the maze. Cade told me it was one of the portals to the mortal realm, this one through water, which I was not a big fan of really. I knew how to swim, or at least I remembered that I knew how to swim, I just hadn't done it after I first came to the academy. Actually, maybe I hadn't done it since I was a little girl.

Cade squeezed my hand, obviously sensing my trepidation of going through the water portal. "It's sort of like going through the abyss when you time jump. Same kind of pull."

"Except, in the abyss, I won't drown."

"You won't drown here either." Ren stepped up next to me. "No one would let that happen. Just go with the flow." He dove into the clear blue pool, disappearing after one small splash of his feet when he kicked downward.

Lucian jumped in next, followed by Jasmine and Georgina.

"I'd rather walk through fire," I confessed.

"Yeah me too. But this is the portal we need to take to get to Pecunia."

"All right, let's do it."

Before I could change my mind, I jumped into the water. Thankfully, it wasn't as cold as I thought it was going to be. Cade dove in next to me, so I followed his lead into the depths of the dark blue. Within seconds, we entered a whirling dervish, and were sucked through the portal. It was so quick that I didn't worry about not having taken a big enough breath, but the entire time I kept seeing flashes of Melany's face. I was getting used to it by now, so I didn't flinch and risk getting tossed out of the water tornado. Once we were out of it, I followed the others as they kicked up to the surface.

When I came up for air, I saw that we were in a harbor, and the others were climbing up onto one of the piers. As I reached it, Cade helped me up. I felt like a drowned rat—probably looked like one too— but before I could ask how they could stand having their clothes and hair sopping wet, Jasmine dried

Lucian with a touch of her hand. The others came next.

I realized it was because of her strong fire power, so following suit, I dried myself and Cade before she could get to us. It started as a warm tingling sensation deep inside my belly, then radiated outwards to the very tips of my fingers.

A grin captured Jasmine's lips when she noticed I'd beat her to it. "Cool, hey?"

"Hell yes. Super cool." I laughed. Part of me wanted to dunk myself back in the harbor, just so I could feel that pleasant, warm, and tingling sensation surging through my body again.

Together, we walked up the docks.

Some people who were there on their boats gawked at us. "They're from that academy for the Gods," a woman whispered.

"I remember that blue-haired girl," a man added.

"More trouble than their worth, in my opinion," another woman concluded.

I turned to see who had said that, but was only faced with a few cool measured stares.

Leaning into Cade, I made a face. "I thought the general public liked us?"

"They do," he responded without a second thought.

"That's not the sense I'm getting here."

With a furrowed brow, his gaze followed mine. "Yeah, I think you might be right."

Before either one of us could mention it to the others, they had all unfurled their wings and were lifting into the air.

"Stay in a tight formation," Lucian called back, his voice wary. Maybe he had noticed the same unease I'd felt.

Cade's wings unfolded—my heart never failed to skip a beat when they did—and he wrapped an arm around my waist, taking us to the sky. I wanted to give him a smacking kiss but refrained. I didn't want to distract him from not letting me plunge to my death.

"Hang on," he said, "It's just a quick flight to Pecunia."

As we flew over the town and then the countryside, I marveled at the view. This part of Greece was quite beautiful and peaceful. A far cry from the constant buzzing of London city, which I still missed greatly, but this had its charms too.

Every now and then, I spotted craters in the ground, downed trees and remnants of the war that had nearly razed the area. New trees and grass had grown, and new buildings had been built in their place. Life had forged on, as it should.

When we neared the impressive temple to Zeus though, I couldn't help but notice a new and different type of war being fought. The bright colors of graffiti sprayed against the usually pristine white marble were shocking, as well as the insidious damage down to the columns and the stairs leading up to the pantheon.

It was an attack against the Gods and everything they represented.

After landing just below the temple steps, several people who had been nearby, gawking at the scene, came running over to us. Most had smiles on their faces, but there were a few disapproving mugs in the crowd.

The police tape that stretched across the columns to keep the public out of the temple, for now, fluttered from our arrival. Two of the officers who stood guard while the maintenance crew was busy trying to get the paint off the marble, came over to talk to Lucian—probably sensing that he was the leader. They weren't wrong. He really seemed born for that role. From what I'd learned about him, I thought that was likely true.

He shook the officers' hands, then asked about what had happened at the temple. The larger of the two, who had identified himself as the captain, immediately spewed the details. The way he prattled on, made me think he very well may have had a slight man crush on Lucian.

"The vandalism happened between one and two a.m. There is usually security in the temple, but the guard who was on duty received an anonymous phone call that urged him away from the area."

"They knew his routine," Lucian concluded.

The captain nodded. "They also knew his cell phone number, so we are looking into anyone who has a beef with the Gods in the security company."

"Has anything like this happened here before?"

"No. Pecunia is usually a pretty quiet and tight-knit community. I mean, we've been through a lot together. But I've heard that attendance at the temple has been down in the past year."

While Lucian continued to talk to the cops, and the others were looking around the building, I decided to mill about within the crowd. Since I didn't have wings, I looked normal, like any twenty-something young woman trying to figure out her life. I had the stringy hair and dark circles under my eyes to prove it.

A cute little girl gushed about the team, one hand in her mother's, and the other pointing at Georgina while saying how awesome her metal arm was.

"She's pretty cool, hey?" I said to her.

She nodded.

"Do you like the Demigods?"

"Yes, I can't wait to go to the academy. I'm going to be a strong and good fighter, just like the Dark Angel."

"Who's that?"

She swung around, gesturing in the other direction, toward the town square. Squinting, I could see a large statue erected in the middle, so I started to walk over there, suddenly drawn to it. Cade's voice called my name in the distance, but I didn't stop until I was right at the base of the glorious sculpture.

My gaze travelled all the way up at the woman immortalized in dark stone. I knew that face. Lately, I'd been seeing it in my dreams and in sudden flashes during the day. Melany Richmond, an imposing figure, especially in stone.

As I craned my neck to regard her, a flash, a flicker out of the corner of my eye caught my attention. I turned to find a door opening in the air, beside the statue. Through that door, I saw her again, a very deep scowl on her pale scarred face.

CHAPTER FIVE

NICOLE

"Υou again? What the hell do you want from me?" Her voice sounded clearer this time. It was as if she was standing right in front of me, and not talking to me from some other dimension or the like.

"I have no idea, mate. I was just going to ask you the same thing." My eyes roamed her face curiously. I had no clue what was going on, but I wasn't scared.

"I'm not the one who opened this portal, or whatever this is." She eyed me suspiciously, fingers twitching.

My gut told me I should be weary of her—I'd

heard the stories. I knew she wasn't a Demigod to be trifled with. I was about to argue with her, but I figured she had me there. Likely, I was the one doing this—not consciously—but for what purpose? It was hard to guess.

"Where are you?" I asked, looking around her for clues. "Or… when are you? I don't really know what's going on."

Melany's face scrunch up with a confused, slightly accusatory look. "What do you mean, where am I?"

"Well, I'm in Pecunia, and from what I've been told, you're… you're, um…" Crap. If she was dead and didn't know it, I sure didn't want to be the one to break it to her. That knowledge might do something to her psyche, so I didn't want to be the cause of someone having an afterlife melt down.

"I'm what?" Her brow furrowed even deeper. She cocked her head, her gaze narrowing in on me like a laser. "What aren't you telling me?"

Should I say something? Maybe she didn't know that she was… dead. Oh, man. Surely there was someone better qualified to give her the news. And if she was actually dead, that still begged the question, where on earth was she, and what was I seeing right now?

Before I could answer her, and possibly do a bunch

of damage I had no interest in doing, Cade's voice came from behind me.

"Nicole? What are you doing over here?"

As I whirled around to face him, I saw the portal vanish from the corner of my eye, shrinking into a tiny blip in the air, then popping out of existence. I blinked at the sudden emptiness, curious and perplexed.

Cade gave me a look, both cautious and a little confused. "Who was that?"

I shrugged. Normally, I liked telling him things, and I knew I could tell him anything, but something inside of me was making me hold back. "What? Don't know what you mean."

"It looked like you were talking to somebody. I thought I saw someone…"

"Nope. You must've imagined it." My teeth sank into my lip. I knew I wasn't fooling him, and sure enough, his eyes narrowed.

"Nic, I can sense something's going on. You can tell me anything, you know that, right?"

Meeting his gaze, I gave him a small, sad smile. "I know."

So why wasn't I telling him about seeing Melany?

I supposed it was because he was under the impression that everything was okay now that my molecules had been fused back together, and that we'd destroyed the Corpse King. That we were happy and normal now, or as normal as the two of us could ever be.

But I didn't really feel fused back together.

There was something, not necessarily *wrong* but out of place. Like I'd been rearranged in the wrong order. All the parts were there, nothing missing, just instead of placed as one, two, three, four, inside me, it felt more like they were one, three, two, four and the number ten for shits and giggles.

Could that be what was causing me to think about Melany all the time? And why I was randomly opening portals to Gods knew where? Because it was still undetermined in my mind where Melany actually existed in this world. If at all.

"What did the authorities say about the vandalism?" I asked, hopefully effectively changing the subject.

His brow furrowed, saying he knew exactly what I was doing, but he didn't press, for which I was grateful.

"They don't know much, to be honest. It happened when the usual security guard wasn't in place, he'd been called away from the area."

"So, an inside job."

"Looks like it," he agreed, nodding.

"I roamed around the crowd to get a bead on the mood of the people. Some are still enamored with the

Gods, but I did hear some discourse. It seems not everyone is as on board with them as they used to be."

"The authorities told us that this wasn't an isolated incident. There have been other vandalism cases across the country."

"Coordinated, do you think?"

"Possibly."

"Did they hit only Zeus's temples?"

Cade shook his head. "Nope, others as well."

"So, it's safe to say this isn't just about old supreme dickhead."

A few chuckles escaped him at my name for Zeus. I had other names for him, harsher names, ones with a lot of colorful euphemisms, but I kept those to myself.

Wondering why I was opening portals to the Dark Angel of Pecunia, I looked up at the statue. It wasn't like I had any connection to her. I didn't know her. She came to the academy after my time. I was in London with amnesia while she'd been here, being a bad ass and disrupting the world of the Gods.

"Did you know her?"

Cade's head tilted to look at the monument. "No, not personally. After finishing my training, I went to live in Olympus. We really didn't hear about much up there. It was very isolating, which I suppose is the point.

I heard about her, certainly. I mean, she took down the most powerful Gods in history."

"She must've been extraordinary to be able to do that."

"Word was she possessed all the attributes of the Gods, even Hades. She had every power and was strong with them."

"What really happened to her, do you know?"

"The official statement is she died in a battle with Nyx, defending the Fates."

"What's the unofficial statement?"

He shrugged. "I don't know."

"Why are you asking about her?" A new voice came from behind us, and it didn't sound friendly.

I whipped around to see that Lucian and Jasmine had joined us. Georgina and Ren were also crossing the square to the spot where we stood by the statue.

"I was just curious about her, that's all. She's a legend."

I could tell that Lucian found it difficult to talk about her still. In some ways, I felt bad for Cassandra, having to exist in Melany's shadow. Although, she didn't seem bothered by it on the couple of occasions we'd talked about Lucian and Melany. It was obvious that Cassandra had liked and respected her, and she really loved Lucian. I hoped that was reciprocated, because she sure deserved someone to be madly in love with her.

"What do you want to know?" Jasmine asked. She wasn't as guarded as Lucian, so maybe my questions would be better directed toward her. We'd built up a bit of a rapport even as she chased me around the field with a sharp spear, threatening to poke me in the ass.

I thought about asking if they thought she was truly dead, but I suspected that would've opened up all kinds of still healing wounds. It also would've opened up a line of questioning to me, and the curiosity of why I was so adamant about needing to know. However, I wasn't ready to talk about that just yet, I just wanted to find out why first, before I discussed it with anyone.

I'd ask my real questions to Jasmine later, when we weren't around Lucian.

"Would she have gleefully poked me in the back with the spear as hard as you do?"

My question must've taken everyone off guard, because they all started to laugh. Even Lucian.

Grinning, Jasmine nodded. "Probably harder."

It was just the right thing to happen to break the tension that had filled the air. I was still feeling my way around Lucian and the others, despite us going through near annihilation together, there was still an awkward distance between us. Perhaps they thought I was somehow trying to replace Melany in their crew, even though I knew that was impossible.

Besides that, I didn't want to be the "new" Melany, I wanted to be current Nicole. I figured I was good enough to be part of their group as I was. I thought I was pretty cool... or at least Cade thought so. And if I were honest, his opinion was the only one that truly mattered to me anyway.

Turning my attention to him now, as he engaged with the others, I watched him. I loved the aristocratic bump on his nose, and the slight dimple in his right cheek when he smiled. His dark eyelashes were impossibly long, and it made me jealous. He may not have been the golden Adonis like Lucian was, but he was strong, smart, kind, and nerdly sexy, so I loved him for that.

Suddenly feeling overwhelmed with emotion, I slid my hand into his. Thinking about Melany and her loss to Lucian, her friends and the academy made my chest tighten. I was so thankful that I'd escaped that fate with the help of Cade and these people standing in front of me.

His gaze focused on me. "You good?"

I nodded. "I'm good. But can we go home now? I need a nap and I really miss Tinker."

"Yeah, we can go." He squeezed my hand. "I'm

pretty sure we got the information Prometheus wanted." His attention shifted to Lucian. "Your call."

"Yup, let's get back to the academy." His gaze tracked the area and caught the same thing I did at the exact same time.

As we were preparing to leave, a small group of about five middle-aged men approached. There was something about the way they moved together, with quick sideway glances at one another, that made the little hairs on my arms stand to attention.

My grip tightened on Cade's hand. "I think trouble is coming our way."

His gaze moved over to the small group that was now crossing the street toward us.

One of the men waved. "Hey, hey. Are you some of those Demigods from the academy?"

By now, the others had also perked up in response to the charged air around us. Something didn't feel right, and I wasn't the only one experiencing the same sensation. Discreetly, Lucian gestured us, and we all kind of formed a defensive line as the mob got closer. And mob was exactly how I saw them. Being on the streets in London, especially a girl alone, I learned really quick how to identity a group of people who were going to become a problem.

These guys were definitely going to be a problem.

"We are," Lucian answered, hands flexing at his sides.

Part of me wondered if he was preparing to create some fire, because my fingers were itching for it. The tips tingled as my fire bloomed to the surface.

Cade squeezed my hand again, giving his head a slight shake. "Not now," he murmured lowly.

"If these jerks start something, I'm not going to back down."

"We can't be seen fighting with mortals, Nic. It would just prompt more disgruntled behavior from them."

The four men spread out a little, one of them looked like he was going to circle us. That would've been a bad move on his part. The one who had initially spoken seemed like he'd been in the army at some point with the way he looked and acted. He took a stance in front of Lucian, who he obviously identified as the leader of our merry band of Demigods.

"What are you doing here?" he asked.

"Just trying to find out what happened to the temple," Lucian answered.

"Right."

"I recognize you from the news on TV," one of the other men said to Lucian, and tipped his chin toward Melany's statue. "With her."

"Yeah, you probably saw a report about how we saved this town, and the country, from destruction."

Ooh, good burn, Lucian. I almost said that out loud, but I bit down on my lower lip so I didn't succumb to the urge to put these guys in their place.

The man sneered, clearly disliking Lucian's response to his jeer.

"Look, we need to get back to the academy, so was there something you wanted?"

The main guy shook his head, a nasty leer on his wide face. "Nope. Just wanted to come over and say hi. Let you know that we recognize who you are and where you're from."

That was most definitely a threat.

The rest of our team agreed, and Jasmine's stance instantly changed. She looked like she did when we were training for battle on the field. Georgina rotated her shoulder, the metal of her arm glinting in the bright sun that cascaded over the town square.

"We'll be sure to keep your faces in our minds as well." Lucian tipped his head. "Have a good day, gentlemen." He made a big show of unfurling his giant wings, stretching them out far, like a bird of prey would do if threatened.

Pairs of powerful white wings opened up all around me, and I felt extremely inferior in the middle of the menacing flock. It couldn't be helped. Resigned, I wrapped my arms around Cade's neck, and with one powerful flap we were airborne.

When I glanced down at the mob as we flew away, I suspected that wouldn't be the last we saw of them. I also suspected that they had everything to do with the vandalism on the temple, and that it wouldn't be the last time that happened...

This was just the beginning.

CHAPTER SIX

NICOLE

*W*hen we returned to the academy, we met with Prometheus—all of us crowded up on his tower platform. I stood farthest away from the edge because I always felt like I was going to fall off, and plummet helplessly to the ground without either my real wings or my metal ones.

We told him what we found out about the vandalism at the temple, and about the mob of men who confronted us in the town square. The news seemed to trouble him greatly, which in turn, made all of us a bit nervous. It was never a good thing to see someone who you considered invincible, concerned about a situation.

I glanced at Cade, noticing he had the same nervous look on his face that I felt. It made my gut tighten, knowing that my nerves weren't mine alone.

Prometheus had stopped pacing, and now stared out the floor to ceiling windows of his office, toward the woods and lake on the east side of the school.

"We need to be monitoring this situation," he finally informed. His voice sounded gravelly and serious but revealed nothing more.

"Do you think it will get worse?" Lucian asked, although I suspected he knew the answer as we all did, and it made my stomach tighten further.

There had definitely been a different energy in town. A low-grade thrum of something developing. Like the electricity in the air that came before a huge, destructive thunderstorm, the water gathering in a cup that will spill over, or the pure, deep stillness before a category five tornado.

Prometheus turned around to look at us. "Yes."

"I don't think we can monitor the situation from here," Lucian suggested, and I was glad that someone was trying to say what we were all thinking. "I'd like to put together teams to position in various areas of the mortal realm."

For a moment, I thought the Titan might disagree, but then he nodded, seeing the logic in Lucian's suggestion. "Put together three teams. But you need to stay undercover. No one should know that you are Demigods."

"That would leave Lucian out then," Cade suddenly added. "He is very recognizable."

Lucian frowned, clearly insulted. "I have to be part of the reconnaissance."

"Cade's right." Rubbing a hand over her face, Jasmine sighed. "Those men recognized you right away."

"In Pecunia," Lucian countered. "I can take a spot somewhere else. I can stay hidden."

Prometheus's hand lifted to stop anymore arguments, making us all fall silent. "I agree that you need to be in charge and on the ground Lucian, but yes, stay out of the public eye. You have a lot of good people who are strong leaders. Use them."

"Are you really concerned that a bunch of mortals can hurt the Gods?" I had to ask. It just seemed so strange to me. The Gods were powerful, immortal. Well, I guess not completely unkillable, or Melany wouldn't have been able to end so many of them. However, she hadn't been mortal. She'd been the strongest of all the Demigods.

"I have seen war before, Nicole. I know what signs to look for."

"But that was between the Gods." He wasn't telling us something here. Something vital. I could feel it all the way to my bones.

"There are a lot more of them than there are of us." His face revealed nothing.

Straightening my spine, I stepped forward. "Sure, but—"

He turned away from me, effectively dismissing me. "Go. Form your teams," the headmaster ordered Lucian. "Let me know when you are ready to dispatch them to the mortal realm." Giving us his back, he went to sit behind his huge desk, moving incredibly gracefully for such a large being. It was a very effective dismissal, so we all filed out of his office silently.

When we were back on the ground, Lucian gestured to me. "What was that about?"

I shrugged, not liking the commanding tone in his voice. "I don't know. I think he's not telling us something."

Actually, I knew it, I just didn't know how.

"Maybe you're just paranoid," Jasmine added gently. "Although you have reason to be, considering everything that's happened to you."

"We all should be paranoid," I snapped in return,

my hackles rising. "When have the Gods ever been completely truthful?"

Glancing at each other, they considered it. Georgina nodded. "She's right."

"That may be," Lucian countered, all doom and gloom. "But I trust Prometheus. I don't think he'd deliberately put any of us in danger."

His blind trust made me want to snort-laugh. Maybe it was because of the way the Gods had once kicked me out and brutally wiped my memory, but I wasn't capable of such blind devotion. "But isn't that the purpose of the academy? To put us all in danger?"

Cade's warm touch reached my arm. "What's going on, Nic?"

Shaking my head, I rubbed a hand over my face. "I'm sorry. I'm still tired, I guess." I looked at everyone. "Don't mind me. I just need to sleep for another few years."

"Don't sweat it." Lucian gave me a rare, friendly smile. "You've been through a lot so I don't expect you to join any of the teams. You still need to rest and get your strength back."

"I think what you're saying is that I'm a weak ass." I chuckled.

Lucian made a face. It looked like he didn't quite know how to react.

"Chill, mate." Playfully, I punched him in the arm. "I'm the first to admit I still need some training before I'm at your level."

After a second, he chuckled with me.

"I wouldn't necessarily say that." Cade swung his arm around my shoulders. "Your fire power is definitely stronger than mine."

Jasmine nodded. "Mine too."

With a shake of my head, I waved a hand at the group. "No worries. You don't need to feed my ego. I know I'm the weakest link in the chain, and I'm cool with that."

The truth was, I was glad to not be part of the reconnaissance teams. I DID need to rest and gather my strength, so I was happy to have that chance. There was also the need to figure out why I was opening those strange portals and seeing Melany. I couldn't do that if I was playing soldier in Pecunia.

Once we left Prometheus's Hall, Cade went with Lucian and the others to prepare for the mission. I told them I was going to go work with Hephaistos in the forge, making some new weapons and such, but in truth I was going to track down Cassandra to see if she could answer my questions about Melany and her demise.

Cade kissed me long and hard—it would've been

embarrassing if it hadn't been so hot—then promised he would come to my room later to fill me in on what had been decided and planned. They all headed one way while I went toward the far wing, where the forge was. Once the others disappeared around the corner, I stopped walking, taking a different corridor toward the infirmary. Hopefully, Cassandra was still there, helping Chiron with potion inventory.

A conversation echoed when I reached the infirmary, so I stopped at the doorway. It wasn't Cassandra or Chiron. It was Iris.

I thought she'd been sprung from the infirmary and was on her way back to Olympus. Maybe her injuries hadn't healed enough in Chiron's mind. Either way, she was still here, chatting with someone in there.

"I'm trying not to think about it. Chiron says for me to heal my body, I also have to heal my mind. My anger isn't healthy."

There was a pause, and I thought for sure there would be another voice, but she just continued talking as if someone had responded to her already. A voice in her head, maybe?

"Maybe. But I don't want to think about that right now. I want to be better. I do. I want to move on with my life."

Again, there was another long pause. Was there

someone speaking and I just couldn't hear them? It was possible, my hearing had been damaged during the whole getting vaporized incident, and that was my one sense that seemed to sputter out every now and then.

"I get what you're saying, but I don't know… I have to think about it."

Who was she talking to? I couldn't stand it any longer; I had to know.

Carefully, I peered around the corner and into the room. Iris was sitting up on her cot, her hands folded primly in her lap. A couple of candles flickered on the table beside her, casting a soft glow around her. As far as I could tell, there wasn't another patient in a cot on either side of her, and there wasn't anyone sitting in the chairs next to her bed either. There was a chair in the shadows, but I couldn't see a form on it.

Maybe the person was standing away from her cot, and just out of my eyesight. My curiosity got the better of me, and I stepped all the way into the infirmary.

Her head shot up the moment I did. "What are you doing here?"

Before I responded, I took some time to scan the room. There was no one else there, so I moved closer to her. "I was looking for Cassandra. I heard she was here helping Chiron with some inventory."

"Well, as you can see, she's not here."

"Do you know where she went?"

"No. And why would I? She's not a friend of mine."

I eyed her, taking in her pale, scarred face. She was avoiding my gaze, which wasn't necessarily out of character, but in the past, she'd liked to glare at me with venom. Some of her venom seemed to have leaked out of her over the past few weeks.

When I was healing in the infirmary, after almost disintegrating into dust molecules, I felt like we'd made some kind of peace, but I knew it was tenuous at best. Maybe that was why she was behaving so timid right now. She didn't want to rock our precarious boat.

"Who were you talking to?" I asked.

"No one." Her gaze lifted and bore into me. Ah, there was the good old Iris I knew and loathed. "Were you spying on me or something?"

"No, I just heard you talking when I approached the door, and I stopped because I didn't want to intrude on your conversation."

She sniffed. "Well, you're intruding now."

That wasn't an answer. That was a deflection. I supposed I didn't blame her for not wanting me to know she was talking to herself. It was normal for people to mutter to themselves, but not necessarily to have a full-blown conversation with questions and answers inside their heads. Cade told me he thought Iris had suffered some kind of mental breakdown over the years.

"Sorry. I'm leaving. But if you see Cassandra again, can you tell her I need to talk to her?"

Giving me a little hum, she nodded her head. Although, I didn't believe she'd tell Cassandra a thing.

As I turned to leave, Chiron came trotting into the infirmary, his hooves making loud clicks on the recently waxed tile floor.

"Nicole? What are you doing here? Are you hurt... again?"

"Nope. I'm good." I shook my head. "All my parts are fused back together. Basically." Grinning cheekily at him, I watched him shake his head and roll his eyes. "I was just looking for Cassandra. I thought she was here."

"She was, and now she's gone." His four legs took him into the room, his sharp gaze roaming over Iris, then back to me. Surely, he was trying to figure out if I'd disturbed his patient enough for him to get pissed about it.

"Do you know where she went? It's kind of urgent."

He shrugged. "She complained about having a headache. I gave her something for it, so I assume she went to sleep it off."

"Okay, thanks." Turning, I began to leave then stopped. "Um, where's her room?"

"I'm pretty sure it is in Athena's Hall."

With a thankful nod, I left. Once in the corridor, I spun in a circle, trying to figure out exactly where that was. I still had a lot of catching up to do on the academy. Most of my memories had returned, but there were still some missing. Like, exactly where every hall was located.

Finally choosing a direction, I started walking, until the feeling that I was being watched swept over me. My steps halted and I whirled around, but there was no one there. Just the shadows creeping along the walls. I peered into the darkness to make sure there wasn't anyone lurking inside, then continued. Unfortunately, that sensation crawled all over me until I reached the large stone staircase and descended.

CHAPTER SEVEN

CADE

The strong suspicion that Nicole was hiding something from me was unshakable.

Actually, I was certain of it. Although she probably thought she was doing a good job at keeping it from me, she had 'tells', and I knew her well. Nicole tended to answer questions quickly with one word and avoided meeting my gaze when she was hiding something important. I just couldn't pinpoint exactly what it was, and the fact that she felt the need to keep something from me felt greasy in my gut.

Something to do with her time powers I would guess. Even though Chronos had saved her life up in the mountain, and she'd spent time in the infirmary healing under Chiron's watchful eye, she hadn't fully dealt with it all. Nicole was warier than usual, and that was saying something. When I tried to talk to her about it, about what she went through, she always said she was fine. Yet, I didn't like that she was cutting me out.

How could anyone be completely fine after experiencing something like that? Not even someone as strong as Nicole could come out on the other side unscathed, physically or mentally. She'd healed from one, but not the other. I really wanted to help her, I ached to, but I could sense her pushing me away a little.

Maybe this separation would be a good thing for us. She needed time to heal, but she obviously needed space as well. Still, it hurt to think that she needed space from me.

Crossing my legs, I sat down on the soft green grass of the west training field, beside Georgina and Mia, while savouring the crisp, earthy scent of the freshly cut blades. There were others gathered. Some I knew well, like Ren and Diego, but the others I barely recognized or knew their names. Lucian and Jasmine stood in front of us, giving the lowdown on what the plan was going to be for their reconnaissance trip to the mortal realm.

"I've gathered the lot of you here for a specific

mission." Lucian's commanding voice rippled over us, his statement causing murmurs among the small crowd.

"We got word that there was some damage and vandalism done to a few of the temples in the mortal realm, so Prometheus sent a few of us to check it out. What we've been able to ascertain is that a few of the Gods' temples had been graffitied and damaged in Pecunia, Kios, and New Athens. There might be more incidents but that was all the authorities were able to tell us."

"That's never happened before," a girl with short black hair stated.

I didn't really know who she was, but I thought her name was Jia. I'd seen her at the stables, helping to train the fire horses.

"As far as we know, it hasn't," Lucian answered.

"What does Prometheus think is going on?" an unfamiliar guy asked.

"He's not sure, but he is worried." Jasmine looked at everyone. "Which is why he's sending us back to do some reconnaissance."

"We will be splitting into three squads, each one going to Pecunia, Kios, and New Athens respectively," Lucian continued, taking up the mantle. "Our mission is to watch and listen. The vandalism in these towns makes it clear that people are not happy. Our job is to find out why, and who is orchestrating these attacks. It could be separate groups, emboldened by each other, or organized by a leader. Either way, the more intel we can gather, the more we can get a handle on it." His gaze traveled over everyone sitting on the ground.

"Do you think this is an uprising?"

"We don't know that yet, Diego," Jasmine cautioned.

"Why would they be angry at the Gods?" a girl with short blond hair inquired. "That doesn't make any sense."

"That's what we need to find out. If the people in these towns have legitimate concerns, we need to know so we can address them. Our job is not only to fight against forces of destruction and keep mortals safe, but to be representatives of the academy."

Prometheus's voice almost seemed to surface in Lucian's words, probably because that was the job he'd been assigned as the face of the Demigods Academy. It was a good face, mind you. Not just good looking, but one that exuded authority and strength. People listened to Lucian, and I hoped it would be enough to keep the peace in the other realm.

I sensed something was brewing… we all did.

"Jasmine and I will each be in charge of a team.

And the other will be under Cade's watch." Lucian gestured to me.

Surprised, I glanced at him. *What the heck?* When he arched an eyebrow at me, I knew I didn't have a choice in the matter. It was best to pretend like I knew what I was doing. Getting to my feet, I joined him and Jasmine at the front.

"Some of you don't know Cade, but he's been a Demigod longer than we have." Lucian smacked me in the back. "He is the smartest person I know and has been working on several secret projects on Olympus for years."

Their eyes widening, some of the recruits regarded me with awe and respect. Not that I needed either, but it was good to have in this situation. These people wouldn't follow me if they didn't know who I was. Lucian vouching for me was a smart tactical move, though his kind words didn't exactly give me warm fuzzies—he had an ulterior motive.

I leaned into him. "Are you sure about me leading a team?"

"Absolutely." Shading his eyes, he looked out over the assembled crowd. "You are a leader, Cade. You were the one who found Nicole, making a plan to rescue her and defeat The Corpse King."

"What's with the secret projects?" I asked, bracing my hands on my hips.

"Gives you an air of cool mystery. Like a spy. Who doesn't want to follow James Bond into an adventure?" He winked.

Rolling my eyes, we both turned back to the group as Lucian resumed his speech, pointing at various people sitting on the grass. "Okay, so here are the assignments. Mia, Ren, and Charlotte will be with Jasmine. Georgina, Marek, and Jia will be with Cade. And Diego, Rosie, and Ezra are with me."

Swift relief coursed through me to have at least one person that I knew. Georgina nodded to me, and I smiled in return.

"Every one of you has certain skills that will be beneficial to your group. I made sure that every team has someone adept at healing as well. Just in case."

"Are you expecting casualties?" Diego asked, concern furrowing his large brow. A good question.

Lucian's attention briefly went to Jasmine and me. "I hope not, but we did experience some hostility when we were in Pecunia. A small group of men confronted us at Melany's statue in the square."

"What did they want?" the girl named Charlotte pressed.

"It was a threat," I blurted out before anyone else could say anything.

Lucian's brow furrowed, letting me know he was not pleased that I'd shared that, but I didn't care. "Now, we can't be sure…"

"You know as well as I do, that it was a threat." I didn't want him to lie to the recruits, or dumb down the situation. Everyone needed to know what kind of danger we were all going into, or we would be leading our people to their unnecessary deaths. "Some mortals are angry with the Gods, and with us. We don't know why, yet. But you should all be on your guard."

Swallowing past his irritation with me, Lucian took a step forward to stand beside me. "Cade is right. There is a level of danger here. Mainly, because we don't know exactly what's going on, and we need to be ready for anything at all times."

"If we're attacked…" Diego got to his feet, stretching out his thick body with audible cracks, "do we retaliate?"

His question prompted everyone to also rise. As Demigods, we didn't shy away from conflict.

"If we are attacked, we are to defend ourselves. But remember, we have powers that the mortals don't. So, using hand to hand combat, and defensive moves, are our best options. The last thing we need is one of us wounding or killing someone unnecessarily with a blast of fire or water."

I glanced at Lucian and leaned into his ear. "I apologize if I overstepped."

Another strategic move. I wasn't actually sorry, but I needed to make the gesture.

He shook his head. "No, you were right in telling them the whole truth. Sometimes I forget that everyone here is a trained soldier, and they deserve to know what they are up against. Zeus and the other Gods often kept things from all of us, as you well know. I don't want to be like that."

"You're not, Lucian. You never have to worry about that." Offering a tight smile, I nodded.

"Let's break into our teams and go through some basic hand to hand and defensive training," Lucian instructed, and a few recruits groaned at that.

"Don't make me pull a Heracles and knock all of you on your asses for that."

Once we all formed our teams, I formally met Marek and Jia. It turned out that Marek had superior water powers and was good with a bow and arrow, while Jia had an affinity to wildlife, including the magical beasts in the stables, and she was an expert knife handler. Also, according to Georgina, she could kick anyone's ass.

I quickly learned that was true, when we were practicing hand-to-hand combat and she flipped me over onto my back, pressing her foot against my neck. Jia was little but extremely strong. Her appearance was unassuming, which would work to our advantage in Pecunia—that was where Lucian thought we'd do best.

He didn't think it would be good for him to be wandering around there, since his face—out of all of ours—was the most recognizable. Georgina would have to stay hidden as well, unless she wore a long-sleeved shirt to hide her metal arm. I, on the other hand, was probably the least recognizable one in all the teams, because I hadn't been part of the battles in Pecunia over the last few years. However, I was starting to feel guilty about that. Perhaps it was why I was eager to prove myself on this mission.

CHAPTER EIGHT

NICOLE

*I*t didn't take me long to find Athena's Hall. It was near the Hall of Learning, which I should've realized, despite the library not existing when I was training at the academy. At one time it had been secret and hidden inside the maze, and not accessible to the average recruit. It was another thing Melany and company had changed.

Thankfully, I did a little peek inside the library before wandering the hall and knocking on random doors looking for Cassandra, because she was there. She sat at one of the long wooden tables with a stack of thick, ancient looking tomes in front of her. That saved me a time-consuming trip.

"Hey." I plopped down in one of the fancy, high-backed chairs beside her.

"Hi." She didn't look up from the book she was reading.

"What are you doing?" My eyes scanned the titles of the books—*The Healing Power of Crystals. 101 Ways to Heal. Divination for Dummies.*

"Trying to discern why I keep having headaches. The potions Chiron gives me aren't doing anything anymore, and the pain is becoming quite annoying." Looking up from the lines of fine, faded text, she closed the book and waved it at me. "What are you doing here?"

"Looking for you, actually." Tucking my hands into the pockets of my jeans, I leaned back in the chair.

Cassandra's eyes narrowed, and she eyed me warily. I didn't blame her really. The last time we chatted an ancient zombie king grabbed us, making us jump through time over, and over, and over. It totally sucked. I wouldn't blame her if she never wanted to hang out with me anymore, just in case something like that happened again.

"I need to ask you some more questions about

Melany." My voice remained low, because I didn't want anyone to overhear what I was saying.

A resigned sigh sunk her chest, before she set her elbow on the table and angled toward me. She didn't look surprised. "You saw her once more?"

"Yup, in Pecunia, at her statue when we were there checking out some things for Prometheus."

She frowned. "I wonder why."

"That's what I'm trying to find out. There has to be a reason, right?" I eyed her. "You haven't had any visions, have you?"

"No, not about this." Her features pinched, and I felt a stab of pity as I realized she probably had one of her painful headaches right now.

My eyes narrowed. "But about other things?"

Her answer never came, she just licked her lips. I wouldn't push or pry. If she wanted to tell me, she would. It wasn't any of my business otherwise, not unless she thought she should share.

"Okay, first tough question… What exactly happened to Melany?" I moved on with my inquiries, not wanting her to feel awkward for staying silent.

"What do you mean?" Cassandra rubbed her fingers over her temples as she looked at me, considering.

"Did she actually die?" I knew my question was blunt, but I had to ask it.

Cassandra looked around the library, eyeing a few of the other recruits who were at the tables reading books—none of them looked our way. It was interesting to me that she didn't want anyone to hear us, either. Seeing her scoot her chair closer to me, I leaned in so she was a mere few inches away.

"Yes?" Cocking her head, she arched an eyebrow at me, clearly knowing exactly how strange her answer sounded.

I smirked. "Is that a question? Because mate, I don't know, I wasn't there. I can't tell you."

Another sigh left her. "You have no idea how many times I've wanted to have this conversation with someone. But I could never with Lucian, Jasmine, or even Georgina. They're still grieving, I think. I don't want to open those wounds with claims that might very well not be true."

"You don't think she's dead," I blurted out, suddenly sure. The answer was clear in her eyes.

"She's definitely not in Elysium, where warriors go when they die." She glanced over my shoulder, but I knew she wasn't looking at anyone or anything other than what she saw in her head.

"How do you know?" I cocked my head, curious.

"Assuming there are only dead warriors there, after all."

Her lips pressed together briefly. "Because I've gone to look."

"You can go to Elysium?"

Cassandra's features crinkled. "Sort of. I can go to places in my visions. Like when I took you to see Chronos that first time." Her hand gripped mine, suddenly insistent. "You can't tell anyone. Not even Cade. If Lucian ever found out… I'm not sure he'd forgive me for looking, or for not telling him."

"I won't. You're keeping my secret; I'll keep yours."

"When you saw Melany, were you able to talk to her?"

I nodded. "Yes, this time it was really clear. I could hear her perfectly and she could hear me. I asked her where she was… the look on her face told me that she was really confused by my question. Like maybe she didn't know where that was."

"Did you see anymore details of the room she was in?" Cassandra leaned back in her chair.

"Definitely a library of some sort. Old. Like this one. Lots of books in shelves, expensive paintings on the walls. Decadent, kind of, you know what I mean?"

"Almost sounds like Hades's Hall." She rubbed her mouth, shaking her head. "That can't be possible.

We've been down there. We went through the Underworld to rescue you, actually. No Melany, no Hades."

"Could it be another dimension?" My nose wrinkled while considering it. "I mean, when I took
everyone to Chronos's mountain it wasn't on this realm
of existence."

"Could be. I think the only ones who would know
for sure would be Thanatos and Hypnos. I'm positive
Melany made some kind of deal with both of them.
She sacrificed herself to save the rest of us and the
Fates."

"Okay, so where do I find them?"

Cassandra snorted. "Well, I know Melany had to
see someone die before she was able to talk to
Thanatos."

My body fell back in the chair, defeated. "Bloody
hell, that sucks." I thought for a moment, there had to
be some other way. "What about Hypnos, then? Can I
talk to him in my sleep?"

"Maybe." The sound of her fingers drumming on
the table echoed in the space, her brow furrowing. She
was obviously thinking about something. "I might know
of another way to talk to Hypnos."

"Talk to me, mate. I'm up for anything."

"You'd have to go see Hecate. I'm pretty sure they
are together."

"Hecate, the witch?"

A smile curved her lips, and she nodded. "Melany brought them back together. It was actually pretty romantic, to be honest."

"All right, where do I find her?"

"In Hade's Hall. In the Underworld. She took over when Hades… after he…"

"Died?"

She nodded.

"Are we sure he's dead too, though? Maybe he's in the same place Melany is."

Nodding, Cassandra breathed deeply. "I'd like to think they are together. He did sacrifice himself for her."

Smirking, I shook my head. "I find it so hard to imagine Hades as some romantic hero." I supposed there was something about him. I mean, he kind of had the sexy bad ass, dark and brooding thing going for him. There must've been something redeeming about him, or Melany wouldn't have ever fallen in love with him.

"Okay, so let's go." I bolted up from the chair.

Cassandra's brow furrowed with deep lines. "You want me to go with you?"

"Yes, mate. I mean, I have no idea how to get to the Underworld, and you do." I gestured to the big books in front of her. "Or you can stay here and read ten thousand pages of text. Which I'm positive will only make your headache worse."

She pushed the books away, then stood. "When you put it like that, how could I refuse?"

"Exactly."

Before we could leave, one of the muses—Clio I assumed, since she was the muse of history, although all nine sisters looked exactly alike—told us to put the books back on the shelves where they belonged. Maybe she was the acting librarian for the day. A couple of those books were really heavy, and I nearly dropped one on my foot, but once that was done, we left the Hall of Learning and the academy.

"So, where to?" I asked Cassandra. "I take it it's going to be some difficult trip to find a secret door that's guarded by some fearsome creature that we have to battle, or some shit like that."

"Sort of."

She couldn't have been more cryptic, but I didn't push, knowing she'd tell me eventually or show me. Honestly, I was getting used to crazy stuff just happening. Sometimes you just had to go with the flow, there was no point in fighting it.

I followed Cassandra into the maze, even more curious

about where we were going. For sure, I'd thought the door to the Underworld was going to be in the dark woods surrounding the academy. Maybe at the lake. To my relief, it wasn't, because then Cassandra would've had to carry me there, as I hadn't made a new set of metal wings yet.

What was worse, I wasn't sure Hephaistos was too keen on making another pair for me, considering I lost the last ones he'd helped me make. Part of me thought it had hurt his feelings, not that he'd ever admit to that. Or to having feelings.

After hitting a dead end and having to back track, we continued through the maze—it must've rearranged itself in the past few days—then reached the center and the white gazebo.

"The door to the Underworld is here?" I was beyond surprised.

"I know, weird right? But I knew there was some kind of connection to Hades here in the gazebo. This was where Melany first met him. And I don't think it's a coincidence that you saw her here."

Turning on my heel, I peered into the shadowy parts along the tall hedges. "Where is it?"

"Can you light the cauldrons?"

I jumped at that. I loved using my fire abilities. My hand hovered above the first one, and flames instantly formed. Once I had lit the other three, I went to stand beside Cassandra. "Okay, now what?"

She grabbed my arm and pulled me over a little until we were right between the first two cauldrons. Her finger pointed at the air. "See that shimmer?"

At first, I didn't see what she meant, but when I squinted my eyes slightly, a waver appeared in the air. It had a similar appearance to the effect seen when one of my time portals opened.

"Cool." Moving toward it, I squinted at the spot to make sure it still shimmered. It did. Then I moved even closer and reached out a hand. The tip of my finger brushed up against something solid. A wooden door. "How did you find this?"

"By accident, actually. I come here sometimes to just sit and think, and maybe to learn more about Melany. Be closer to her somehow. I saw it, opened it, went down deep into the earth and ran into one of her old friends."

"Does Lucian know?"

She shook her head. "No. I'm afraid to tell him. I'm afraid that he'll come here and think about her the same way I do."

There was pain in her eyes, and it made me sad. Seeing Lucian and her together, I knew that he had real feelings for her. I didn't want to say love, as that would've been presumptuous on everyone's part, but I could see it between them. I knew that look though. Hadn't I experienced it in some way, watching Cade with Iris all those years ago? It was longing, and I knew how painful it could be.

"I've seen the two of you together. I don't think you have anything to worry about there."

She just nodded.

I reached over and grabbed her hand, squeezing it. "Thank you for showing me the door. You don't need to come with, if you don't want to."

"Well, considering you're going to run into a giant, three-headed puppy, who misses his mistress something awful and likes to bite those he doesn't know, I should probably go with you. Cerberus knows me. He'll be better behaved… I hope."

"All right. Let's do it." Touching the shimmer again, I gripped the metal knob on the door and started to turn it to open.

"Hello, Nicole and Cassandra. What are you doing? And may I be of service?"

I whipped my head to find Tinker rolling toward the hidden door, his gear eyes blinking with curiosity.

CHAPTER NINE

NICOLE

J yanked my hand out of the shimmer and put it behind my back as if I'd been caught finger painting on the walls of my bedroom, which I did do when I was little. "Tink? What are you doing here?"

"I am looking for you, Nicole. And I have found you." He bleeped and blooped, happy about his accomplishment.

"Why are you looking for me?"

"Cade asked me to go find you. He was worried about you." Concern tinged my little creation's voice.

My chest tensed as I glanced at Cassandra. "I guess I'll have to take a rain check on our adventure."

"You were going on an adventure?" Tinker asked wistfully.

I knew he was just a little robot with gears and circuit boards in his head, but I swore that after all the time-jumping we did, he enjoyed it and wanted to do it again.

"Um, not really," I lied.

He blinked at me, and it was almost like he knew I was fibbing and was very disappointed. Or that could've just been my own guilt fluttering around in my belly. Guilt for lying to Tinker, which was basically the same thing as lying to Cade.

Extending my hand toward the cauldrons, I snuffed out the flames with a flick of my fingers. "Okay, let's head back, Tink. Is Cade waiting in his room?"

Blink. Blink. Blink. No bleeps this time. No bloops.

Argh. Guilt. Guilt. Guilt.

"Yes, he is." Tinker looked up at me expectantly, clearly eager to take me to Cade.

A frustrated sigh left me, my plans thwarted by a robot so cute and sweet that it was impossible to be mad at him. "I'll see you later, Cass." I glanced at her regretfully.

She nodded, then opened up her wings and rose into the air.

For a brief moment, I watched her as she flew away. Envy that she could just fly whenever she wanted filled me to the brim while I walked with Tinker through the maze, and out to the path leading back to the academy. The wings of a Demigod were magnificent, and I couldn't help but miss my own.

When we arrived to Cade's room, I knocked on the closed door. It immediately opened to show him on the other side, and smiling, he ushered us inside. Tinker rolled in, making happy bleeps and bloops, but my guilt was heavy, thick, and greasy as it swirled in my gut.

Cade leaned in and kissed me on the cheek. "Missed you today."

Inhaling his scent of metal and skin, I draped my arms around his neck, pulled him in, and kissed him properly, which made his eyes bug out. "I missed you too."

His hands slid in around my waist, rough and strong against my skin. "Hmm, we should part more often."

I made a face, the slightest bit insulted. "That's a weird thing to say."

"No, I mean, if that's the greeting I get for not seeing you for a few hours, then…" he sputtered, and my irritation melted, understanding what he'd meant. Plus, he was so damn cute when he was off his game that it made me laugh.

"I'm just messing with you." Placing a quick kiss on the tip of his nose, I traced one of his unruly eyebrows with the tip of my finger, then turned and collapsed onto his bed, arms splayed out like I was about to make some snow angels on his soft blanket. "Anyway, we got the kid to worry about." I gestured to Tinker, who was rolling around in circles in front of the work bench. "Don't want him to see something he shouldn't."

That made Cade's cheeks flush, which just made him ten times sexier in my eyes. I knew he was thinking about all the things we could do that we shouldn't let Tinker see.

He gestured to the bench instead. "Tink, how about you power down so I can charge your circuits?"

"Yes, Cade, that does sound like a good idea." The little robot stopped moving, a few beeps echoing, then a long whirr as he turned off his cognitive systems. Pulling a couple of power cords from the wall, Cade plugged them into various outlets in Tinker's body.

With a quirk of his eyebrow, he then plopped down on the bed next to me, his lips curved into a sexy smirk. "You were saying?"

I rolled over onto my side so I could look at him. I

grabbed one of his pillows and smooshed it against my belly and wrapped my arms around it. "How was the planning meeting?"

"Lucian asked me to lead one of the teams."

"You sound so surprised."

"I was actually."

In all honesty, I wasn't, so I reached over and grabbed his hand. "I'm not. You'd make a great man in charge. You're the smartest person in this place."

"Intelligence doesn't always make for a good leader." He became pensive, his clever brain was clearly running through all the reasons he shouldn't be in charge.

The doubts he had about himself spread along in his face, affecting the way he held his head and back. The sight broke my heart. He had so many gifts. So many strengths. He could run this academy for the better, in my opinion. Lucian was a leader for sure, but he was a soldier, a lion on the battlefield. Cade was a diplomat and a tactician. He knew how things worked, and how people did as well. He'd be my choice to be headmaster of the academy if anything ever happened to Prometheus.

"Who's in your squad?"

"Georgina, thankfully."

"Oh, I like her. She's cool, and her arm is truly bad ass."

His lips tilted as he smiled. "A guy named Marek and a girl named Jia are also in my group."

"What are they like?"

"Unsure about Marek yet, he seems all right. Jia is tiny but mighty. She kicked my ass during hand-to-hand combat."

I chuckled. "Nice. I like her already."

Yanking me closer to him, Cade fell onto his side and threw his arm over me, cuddling me tightly. "We're going through the portal tomorrow. My team will be stationed in Pecunia."

"Do you know how long you'll be gone?" It was just starting to hit me that we were going to be separated again, but this time, it would be on purpose. I kind of didn't like that. It made a knot of sorrow form in my guts.

"Not sure. I guess however long it takes for us to figure out exactly what is going on."

My eyes lifted to his face, and I studied it, running my finger along his cheek and jaw. He kissed the tip when it reached his mouth.

"Will you miss me?" I asked but hated it a little. I didn't want to sound needy.

"Of course. I miss you right now."

My brows furrowed, and I pulled back a bit. "What does that mean? I'm right here."

"You've been distant. I know something's up, and I don't know why you won't tell me what it is. I'm trying to be chill about it. But obviously, I'm not doing a very good job." His lips tilted into a little smirk.

I sighed. "I didn't want to worry you, Cade."

His eyes narrowed. "Too late. Now I'm even more worried."

"Argh. Don't be. It's not really that serious."

"Just tell me, Nic."

"Fine." A defeated breath left me. "I've been having flashes of Melany in my head. At first, it was just like dreams or random images, but now I'm like, *seeing* her."

His frown deepened. "Like a ghost?"

Laughter burst out of me at that, because I hadn't even really thought about it in that way. Maybe I was seeing her ghost. Maybe that was what this was.

"Why is that funny?"

I sucked in my laughter because I could see that it had offended him. "It's not, not really. Twice now, I've opened a portal to, I don't know… somewhere, and I've talked to her."

"But she's dead."

"I know." Sitting up, I scratched my head, where a deep ache bloomed. My ponytail was starting to hurt, so I took off the hair tie and let my hair fall down to my shoulders. I ran my fingers through it, massaging my scalp a little.

Cade sat up too. "Are you opening a portal to Elysium?"

"I don't think so." I shook my head. "Cassandra said that Melany's not in Elysium. She already looked."

"If she's not there, then…"

I shrugged. "Exactly."

"Why do you think this is happening?"

"I don't know, but I'm sure it means something."

"And you actually talked to her?"

"Yeah. It was really weird. And I don't think she knows where she is either."

Cade's hands lifted to his face, scrubbing the growing tension. "Wow. That's…"

"Right?!" Suddenly, a thought exploded in my head, and I grabbed his shoulders. "Don't tell Lucian. Or anyone actually. I don't want to give hope to them. That would be damaging beyond belief, I think, especially if this is all just some glitch in the Matrix."

"I won't say anything." Taking my hand in his, he squeezed it. "How are you going to figure out what this means?"

"Well…" I scrunched up my face. "I'm going with Cassandra to the Underworld, to talk to Hypnos.

Supposedly, he's shacked up there with Hecate. I guess they're lovers or something like that." The words hurried out of me in one breath, hoping maybe he would not hear some of it, and just accept that I wasn't going to do something silly and reckless... alone.

He let out a long sigh, pursed his lips, then nodded. "You make sure you stay safe. Use all your powers. Even your time jumping. You could wield it like you did that time we were practicing with the bows and you stopped everyone, so you could move around them."

My heart exploded with emotion, and I smiled at him. Sometimes I wondered what I did to deserve a guy like Cade. He just got me.

"I thought you might try and talk me out of it."

A sexy smirk tilted his lips. "I learned long ago that once you have something lodged in your mind, reasoning with you isn't possible."

"Fancy talk for saying I'm stubborn." I pushed out my bottom lip.

His mouth brushed against mine as he leaned into me. "I love your stubbornness."

"I love..." I kissed him back, then drew away to look him in the eyes. "You."

"I love you, too."

I got off the bed for a second, then settled myself down onto his lap, a knee on either side of him. His hands immediately curled around my waist, clutching me there. Cupping his face with my hands, I kissed him again. When I pulled back, I kept his face in my hands and stared into his beautiful eyes.

"Don't you dare get hurt out there."

"I won't. It's just intelligence gathering. We'll be asking lots of questions, watching the temple for activity, noting down any problems. And that's about it. Basically, we'll be glorified temple security guards."

In my head, I knew logically that was all the mission would be, but deep in my gut, swirling around like a tornado was something else. A feeling that it wasn't going to go as smoothly as that. I had felt a lot of tension and anger when we were in Pecunia. The citizens were not happy with the status quo. Discourse was being sowed.

Despite it just being the rumblings of a few mortals, I sensed there was going to be hell to be reaped. The Gods had been in charge for a very long time, and someone, or a lot of someones, were not happy about it. Maybe they thought they needed to change the guard.

Unfortunately, Cade and his team, and the rest of us, Demigods, were going to be right in the middle of that change.

When I kissed him again, it was harder, with a bit

of desperation seeping into the kiss. He must've sensed what I needed, because his hands moved down around the curve of my back end. Cade lifted me up, spun me around, and laid me down on the mattress, his body covering mine.

Surrendering to him, I wrapped my legs around his waist. I didn't want to think anymore, just to feel him, and only him, for as long as possible…

In the morning, he would be off to Pecunia, and I would go down to the Underworld. Something was bound to happen with one or both our missions. Good or bad, I couldn't rightly say. All I knew was that the world we knew, right here and now, was shifting.

CHAPTER TEN

CADE

*T*he next morning, Nicole accompanied us to the cave portal, along with Cassandra. I had wanted to leave her sleeping in my bed—she looked so peaceful, the only time she ever seemed peaceful, to be honest—but she'd insisted.

The whole thing was so odd, like I was off to war. Part of me wondered if she should clip a piece of her hair, so I could take it with me. I'd mentioned that very thing as we said our goodbyes at the edge of the pool, but she smacked me, scowling.

"Hell no, I'm not cutting my hair."

I laughed. I loved getting a rise out of her and

getting to see her more playful side. "It was just a suggestion. Something to remember you by."

"Remember this." Nicole's arms wrapped around my shoulders, and she crushed her mouth to mine. My hands immediately found her waist, and I pulled her close, wishing that I could just kiss her forever.

Kissy noises arose from others, though it was all in good fun. "Ewwww, get a room."

After a final hug and a lingering press of her forehead against my own, Nicole stepped back. "Stay safe. All of you." She looked at Georgina, Jasmine, Lucian, and the rest of the teams.

"You too," I replied sternly.

I still wasn't keen about her going to the Underworld, but she'd survived the Corpse King and nearly getting evaporated. After all that, I knew she was strong enough to handle a giant three-headed dog, and who knew what else that lived in Hades's Hall. Still, it didn't mean I liked the thought of her in danger. The rumors I'd heard about the Furies gave me the shivers.

Lucian was the first into the pool, followed by Jasmine, then the others. Sucking in a deep breath, I jumped in after Ren, and followed him deep into the rushing water to the portal that swirled around, resembling a destructive tornado funnel.

Just like Nicole, I preferred to go through fire than

through water, but I didn't find it terrifying or anything. I knew it would be safe once I was inside it, and I'd end up coming up for air in a bay in another realm. Still, I wasn't fond of the way it felt, the heaviness and the icy cold. I would take sparks of fire over this every time.

Once we were up on the docks, I dried myself while Jasmine helped the others, then Lucian had us separate into our squads. Each was equipped with backpacks full of supplies such as food, extra clothing, and a few weapons, like small knives—because carrying around broad swords and bows would be way too conspicuous. We also took money, which felt weird considering none of us had used money for the last three years, or more.

Each of the team leaders had one other thing in our backpacks, a scrying lantern that Prometheus gave us so we could communicate with him. We only had to light the wick, spin it, and then we would connect with his lantern to see and hear him. It was actually a kind of clever piece of construction and magic. As far as contacting each other, the first thing we were to do was buy cell phones; it would be less cumbersome than everyone having a bulky lantern of their own.

Once we arrived in town, we were to find our command center, which in our case, turned out to be a large apartment in the middle of the city. It was owned and maintained by the Gods—Dionysus to be exact,

since he often went there for some entertainment—
then we would make a plan.

"Also, no flying," Lucian ordered before any of us
could unfurl our wings. "We need to stay undercover,
which means being under the radar."

"How are we supposed to get to Pecunia?" I asked.
It was a ten-minute flight, but I had no idea how long it
would take otherwise.

"There are cars in the parking lot."

"You want us to steal a car?" Georgina sputtered,
and I saw a peek of her wings before she tucked them
back into her body. "That's not right."

With a chuckle, Lucian shook his head. "Of course
not, Gina." His hand dug into his jacket pocket, pulling
out three sets of car keys. He tossed one to me. "You
know how to drive, don't you, Cade?"

"Yeah, of course."

I had gotten my driver's license before receiving my
Shadowbox to the academy. Back home, in Canada, I
used to drive my dad's pickup truck to high school and
back. It would always get really cold there, so we
needed a vehicle, especially in winter. Although, I
hadn't driven in what felt like forever. Part of me hoped
that it was just like riding a bicycle, and when I got
back in a vehicle, it would all come back to me.

Unfortunately, I could honestly say that didn't

happen when I put the key into the ignition of the blue Toyota **YARIS** and started it. I had to sit there for a moment, and adjust to the car before I changed gears and got out onto the highway toward Pecunia.

"Do you want me to drive, Cade?" Marek blurted out from the back seat when the car caught between gears. I was a Demigod, I could fly, I could fight, but clearly, he had little confidence in my ability to maneuver this steel death trap. It was actually pretty funny.

"No, it's fine. I got it." I had gotten us out of the parking lot and onto the highway fairly confidently, and while I did, I thought I might end up having a problem with Marek. He looked at me like I didn't know what I was doing and had no business being in charge.

I really hoped he was wrong.

The drive to Pecunia took about an hour. A relatively short drive, though it seemed like forever compared to how quickly we could have flown. Funny how easily perspectives changed. When we turned off the main road and onto the town square, we passed Zeus's temple, where the vandalism had taken place. As we did, I saw that they had cleaned it all up, so the white stone and marble looked as pristine as always.

There were a few worshipers on the steps that led to the main temple, carrying baskets of offerings like figs, bread, and wine. Everything looked nice and normal. No angry mobs lurking around the corners. We all knew, however, that things weren't always as they seemed.

I drove into the traffic circle that rounded the park where Melany's statue stood. As we went around it, Jia opened the window and popped her head out. "Wow. I hadn't seen it before. I didn't come to the initial unveiling."

"It's unnerving to look at," Georgina admitted. "It looks so much like her."

"It does," Marek agreed.

Coming out of the circle, we passed another street lined with cute shops and restaurants. Soon after, I found the address that Lucian had given me for our hideout, which just happened to be over a pub. So not surprising, considering it was Dionysus's little hide out away from the academy. I imagined him in the pub, drinking and singing every night.

After parking, we went around back, up the staircase, and into Dionysus's place. A fully furnished, two-bedroom apartment with a large sofa, and huge windows overlooking the street. It was actually pretty nice, so it had me wondering if after all of this was done, I should ask Dionysus if Nicole and I could spend a few nights here. Pretend we were just a regular couple on a short holiday.

It would be pretty magical to be here with her, nothing to do but eat, sleep, and be naked together, instead of fighting monsters to save the world.

Once we settled in, I got everyone to sit at the dining table so we could discuss the plan. A plan that I hadn't really devised yet. It was just an inkling of an idea, and I wasn't completely sure it was a great idea.

"Okay, so I think one of the first things we need to do is establish comings and goings at the temple. Study the guards' schedules, and also see who the regulars are there. We could take photos with the cell phones and record the times. Takes notes on those who don't look like they belong there."

"Did Lucian say how long we were going to be here?" Marek asked, his gaze drifting over to the big front windows. It was obvious he really didn't give a crap what I had to say.

"He didn't specify. I imagine we'll be here at least a week so we can establish some patterns. Most people worship at the temple once a week."

Marek nodded, but I felt like he wanted to say something. Something told me we were going to have words sooner rather than later.

"Should we work in shifts?" Georgina asked. "Teams of two would look less conspicuous, don't you think? Just in case others are watching the temple for similar reasons."

"That's a good idea. We can split up into two couples. Me with Jia and you with Marek."

It was hard to pass on the initial urge to pair myself with Georgina, because I liked her and I knew her, but I also knew that I needed her level head and quick thinking on my side. She could handle Marek if there was any problem, which I didn't think there was between the two of them. They seemed to get along well. They had probably fought together in one of the battles.

"Jia and I will go to the temple as if to worship and be on the lookout for anything suspicious. Georgina and Marek, you two will mill about in town, go to the shops, and cafes to get a bead on the locals. Listen for any discourse being spread."

Marek got to his feet. "At least we'll get to eat some good food during this pointless mission."

"What's your problem?" I got in his face. "Why did you even bother coming? I'm sure you could've told Lucian to find someone else."

"It's pointless. If someone is desecrating the temple, then find them and make sure they never do something like that."

"That's what we are doing here, Marek. The point is we don't know who the culprits are. We are here to find out who and why. Why being the most important part of this mission. It could be just some stupid kids, or it could be the start of something bigger. Something bad and dangerous. Which is what Prometheus is worried about."

He shrugged. "I guess."

"Just do your job, okay?"

He nodded. "Yes. Fine."

Georgina patted me on the shoulder. "You're doing good. Don't let Marek rattle you. He's a bit of a know-it-all, but ultimately, he is a good guy who just wants to do the right thing."

"I'll take your word for it." It was the truth, I had to rely on her word because I didn't know Marek. I did trust her though, so that would have to suffice.

Once we all left the apartment, Georgina and Marek went one way, while Jia and I went the other. I suggested that we stop to get a bottle of wine to bring with us. I didn't want to enter empty handed since that would get people's unwanted attention. We had to come off as a couple here on holiday, just paying our respects to the Gods for good weather and good favor.

Wine in hand, Jia and I walked across the town square toward Zeus's temple. When we reached

Melany's statue, she briefly stopped and stared up at it. An odd look spread along her face. It wasn't one of reverence, like I'd seen on a lot of people as they admired the Dark Angel, but maybe consideration or reflection.

"Did you know her well?" I asked, curious.

"Not well, no. We didn't move in the same circles."

I didn't prod any further, it didn't seem like she wanted to expand on that cryptic answer.

We continued on our way, and the closer we got, the more attention I gave to those who were also on their way to the temple, and to those who milled about just outside on the steps. I paid particular attention to any lone males, or those in pairs. Thankfully, I didn't recognize any of those faces from the small mob that had approached us.

Jia and I climbed the stone steps and went inside the shrine. It was bustling with all sorts of people, all eager to gain favor from the mightiest of Gods, Zeus. Little did they know that he wasn't around anymore to grant their wishes. The academy had managed to keep that explosive detail to themselves.

His marble statue sat on a raised altar in the center of the space, extending to twenty feet tall. There were families setting down homemade meals onto the altar, each touching Zeus's feet and uttering prayers. Single women, and men, both young and old, set down baskets of breads and pastries while uttering their hopes for the future—maybe for a child or a loved one. I imagined some of them were there in hopes that their son or daughter would receive their Shadowbox at eighteen, to come to the academy.

We approached the altar, setting the wine down on the white marble near Zeus's right foot. I draped my arm around Jia shoulders and leaned in closer. "See anyone suspicious—?"

A sudden scream pierced the air.

CHAPTER ELEVEN

NICOLE

*O*nce everyone had jumped into the pool and portal, the churning water swallowing Cade whole, Cassandra and I returned to the gazebo in the maze, ready to open the door to the Underworld.

Lighting up the cauldrons again, we stood back to find the mesmerizing shimmer in the heat waves radiating from the flames. It took a few minutes, but I could see it plainly. Without hesitation, I reached into the shimmer and touched the door with the palm of my hand.

"Are you ready?" I asked Cassandra.

"Yup." She lifted her shirt to reveal a couple of

daggers strapped to her waist. Her expression was grim but determined. "The Furies can be a bit bothersome. Gotta be prepared."

I grinned. I liked her more and more every time we got to hang out and do dangerous shit together.

Gripping the handle firmly, I opened the door, but before I could step through it, my name was called from the edge of the hedge.

"Nicole! Wait for me!"

I glanced over to the right to see Tinker wheeling across the grass at top speed toward us.

Sighing, I shook my head and swallowed the flicker of irritation at the appearance of my little robot. I should've guessed that Cade would command Tinker to look out for me. It was both sweet and a bit condescending. As if I couldn't possibly take care of myself. However, I knew that wasn't how Cade looked at it. He knew full well what a badass I was, but he just couldn't seem to help himself.

The little robot rolled to a stop next to me. He couldn't breathe, but if he could, he would have sighed with relief that he'd found me. "I apologize for my late arrival. It took me a bit longer than usual to locate you."

"It's fine, Tink." I patted his dome head. "You're here now, just in time."

Cassandra gave me a concerned look.

"Don't worry, he'll be useful."

"Yes, I will," he added eagerly. "My hand can be turned into a screwdriver, a hammer, a wrench, pliers, and even a laser." He twirled his metal claw around really fast, so much that it was just a blur, then a blue light emanated from it, burning a hole into one of the wooden poles of the gazebo. Curls of black smoke rose in the air.

"That's good, Tink!" I shouted to get his attention as he showed off his mad skills. I didn't want him to burn the whole thing down. "Thank you for the demonstration."

"I also have water and snacks." His front panel popped open to reveal bottles of water and some crisps packets. Cheese and onion, my favorite flavor, of course. I laughed, wondering if adding the distinctly British option had been Cade's idea or Tinker's. It didn't matter, it touched my heart anyway.

My fingers danced over the smooth metal when I patted his head again. "Thanks, mate. Let's do this."

Cassandra stepped through the doorway first, I made Tinker go next, then I went in last. It was pitch black inside, and moving from the light into absolute darkness was disorienting, so I opened my hand and made a globe of orange fire so we could see. The eerie glow illuminated a very steep stone staircase descending into the earth. A shiver rushed along my spine as a puff of cold, stale air blew up the depths, dry and full of rot.

I wrinkled my nose. "Smells like the caves we were in before, with the zombies."

"Yeah." Cassandra's body trembled, and she wrapped her arms around herself. She was a badass with daggers strapped to her waist, but that didn't mean she wasn't stepping into her own personal hell. "I was hoping to never smell that again. Brings back too many bad memories."

Grasping her shoulder, I squeezed it reassuringly. "You don't have to come with me. I'm sure I can find my way."

"No, I'm fine. Believe me, you'll want me with you once we get down to the bottom of these stairs."

She was probably right, and I was secretly happy that she didn't take me up on my offer to bail. I was used to doing these things on my own, but I was also finding that I didn't want that anymore. Having Cassandra with me, made me miss Cade and Pinky less.

Since I held the light, I walked ahead of them. Cassandra came behind me, a hand pressed to one of her secreted daggers while Tinker followed, switching out his wheels for his tractor glide. He had night vision, so he didn't need any light to find his way down the deep stone steps.

I counted the steps under my breath as we moved downward, but stopped after I reached one hundred. The deeper we went, the colder and earthier it got. Vines and tree roots snaked out from between stone blocks. Dry flakes of dirt peppered each of the stairs, and it wouldn't have surprised me if the next step I took had landed on hard packed soil instead of rock.

After about twenty minutes, I finally hit the last stair and walked out into a vast cavern that, when I held out my hand with the ball of fire, looked like it spanned miles. It probably did. I imagined the Underworld was infinite. A never-ending swath of potential horrors.

The last time I was down here, was when we took a boat on the river Styx with the skeletal Charon. That had been frightening, but this was worse. It was probably because I didn't know what was going to be ahead of us, what, or who we were going to run into, and it was just the three of us, not a small army like back then. I missed having Cade beside me. He was most definitely a source of strength for me, and I was just starting to realize that.

"Okay, now where?" I motioned to Cassandra to

point us in the right direction, the orange light I'd created glimmering as I moved.

"If we keep walking, we should run into it." She swallowed thickly, and I knew she wasn't any more eager than I was to move onward.

"Run into what?"

"Hades's Hall. It won't be hard to miss, as it's a huge metal door in a dank dark cave near the river."

"Awesome." I wrinkled my nose.

"Oh, and I'm sure we'll run into Cerberus long before we reach the door. We'll need him to cross the river."

That didn't make me feel any better, but I was sure it wasn't meant to be reassuring.

As we walked together, side by side this time— Tinker prattled on with facts about the Underworld and its inhabitants, including Cerberus. That was not helpful, but he seemed to need to do it. I wondered if it was because he, too, was nervous.

Could robots get nervous?

I thought that this one most definitely could—it became increasingly obvious with how bleak and lifeless this place was. What little life we did encounter was low, scraggily scrub on the ground, and that was about it. There was no sound of any creatures, no chirping of cicadas or scuttling of beetles, no trilling of birds or grunts made by rodents on the ground. The very air felt lifeless, as if there were no water molecules in the air. It was so dry, my skin felt like it was actually cracking, pulling so tightly around my flesh that it couldn't contain it without splitting open.

Looking around at the bleak surroundings, I started to think about Melany again.

"Why would anyone purposely want to be the ruler of all this?" Honestly, I didn't understand what the Underworld had to offer anyone.

"I think Melany saw the beauty of the darkness. She wasn't afraid of it."

"Yeah, I suppose. I hope the hall is not like this."

Cassandra chuckled. "Oh, it isn't. Hades liked opulence and comfort. And heat." She rubbed at her arms.

Calling my fire to the surface of my skin, I threw an arm around her shoulders, to warm her.

"Thanks."

"No worries. You saved my life once, it's the least I can do for you." My lips curved into a cheeky grin, which she returned.

Up ahead, just slightly past the glow radius of my fire ball, I could make out the edge of the river. We were getting close. As if to make that abundantly clear, a series of thuds echoed across the earth toward us.

The sounds neared, and the ground began to shake beneath our feet.

I tried to trick my brain into thinking it was just an earthquake, nothing serious, but I knew in my gut what the thunderous sounds meant. Along the opposite riverbank, a dark shadow grew, flowing directly toward us.

Except it wasn't a shadow. It was a giant, three-headed devil hound with six glowing red eyes.

"Oh crap," Cassandra blurted. "I forgot how big he is."

"Big" was too silly a word for something as colossal and terrifying as the beast that leapt into the deep river, the water just skimming his underbelly while it approached us. Three low rumbles emanated from his mouths.

"Cerberus! It's me, Cassandra. Remember me? I'm a friend of Melany's."

The rumbles turned to loud, scary growls when Cerberus lowered his three large, car-sized heads, and bared three sets of razor-sharp teeth. A line of drool escaped the center, gaping maw, and nearly hit me on top of my head. Gross.

"I don't think he remembers you."

"Cerberus! I'm Melany's friend."

I glanced at Tinker. "Grab my arm." He did.

"Grab my arm or shoulder, anything," I shouted at Cassandra. "I don't care where. Just grab me! Now!"

The second she wrapped a hand over my right shoulder, I snapped my fingers.

Time stopped and everything in it, except for us. Good thing because Cerberus's teeth were mere inches from both Cassandra and me. One more minute and we would've both been puppy chow.

Cassandra's eyes bugged out, her neck craning to find the tip of a fang just about to graze the top of her head. "Holy crap."

A whole slew of bleeps and bloops escaped Tinker, like he was letting out a long string of curses.

She turned to gape at me. "I didn't know you could do this."

"It's one of my fun party favors."

"This is… wow."

"Well, now we need to move quickly because I don't really know how long it's going to last." I looked up at the giant beast in the still water. "How did we need him to get to the hall?"

"We can't cross the river, not with any of our powers. I can't even fly over it. It's impassable."

My eyes narrowed. "But he could've carried us over?"

She nodded.

"Okay, well, I guess we use him as a bridge now."

Her eyes bugged out even more. Tinker's bleep bleep, bloops echoed around us, which was kind of comical, considering, and it made me laugh.

"Maybe you should stay here, Tink. I'm not sure if I can carry you and balance myself at the same time."

"I wish to go with you, Nicole." His little claw hands opened and closed on repeat.

"Are you afraid?"

"Of course I am not afraid. I cannot feel fear."

Except, I was pretty sure he was experiencing it all the same. I couldn't leave him alone. That would've been cruel.

"Okay, we'll figure it out."

The "figuring it out" was that I climbed onto one of the beast's heads, then Cassandra lifted Tinker toward me. Grabbing him, I set him onto Cerberus's neck—he was heavy, but thankfully, we both possessed superior strength. "Can you roll over him from here without falling?"

"Yes. No problem, Nicole." Tinker's arms shot out ahead of him, all the way to the beast's hind quarters, his little claw hands clamped onto its flesh, and he slowly rolled himself forward. There was no way he could fall with those secure lines. Made me wish I could do the same thing.

While I started walking along the back of the fabled Cerberus, Cassandra followed me closely. I swore I held my breath until I reached the tail. When we got there, I looked out over to the other side of the river. It wasn't far, so I figured it could be easily jumped.

"Tink, could you shoot yourself onto the shore?"

He made a few beeps, and I wondered if he was calculating the odds of his success. "Yes. I will reach with my arms like I did to cross the dog's back, and I should be able to hold up my body weight to get across."

"Okay, let me go across first, then I can make sure to catch you."

"Thank you, Nicole."

His metal arms shot out like before, clamped onto the dirt on the shoreline, and he began revving up. Backing up a bit, I took off running, leaping off Cerberus's ass. I landed on the other side without a wobble. Immediately after, Tinker shot himself across the frozen river. He made it without even needing my help.

Cassandra jumped last. And it wasn't a moment too soon, because I could see time and space starting to wiggle in front of me. It wouldn't be long before Cerberus unfroze, figured out where we went and chased after us.

CHAPTER TWELVE

CADE

I whipped around to see who had screamed and spotted a young woman in the corner, not much older than Jia and me. Her hands lifted toward her face, dripping with something red. There were a couple of round crimson marks blooming on her shirt, but I didn't think they were gunshots. I was pretty sure it was paint. I could smell it in the air.

That was confirmed when two men dressed in black stopped across from her, carrying what looked like semiautomatic rifles. Turning, they shot other people nearby.

"Stop worshipping the false Gods!" one of the

thugs yelled at the crowd. Arrogance was painted over his face, so certain was he of his righteousness.

The red paintball hit an older man in the face, splattering all over his skin while his wife got hit in the neck. Both of them cried out, probably both out of fear and pain—that had to hurt. I'd been shot by paint pellets before and it did sting, especially in a spot not padded with muscle or fat.

This just wasn't right. I couldn't believe these thugs were shooting innocent people, even with paintballs.

"Next time, these will be real bullets!"

Across the hall, another two "gunmen" burst into the space, shooting at more people. The chaos and confusion about what was going on caused a stampede out of the temple. I saw an older woman get shoved to the side and feared the worst.

There had been enough mass shootings in the world that the sound of a gun, any gun, in a public space would strike terror into the heart of anyone with a lick of common sense. Even more, I knew first hand what a group of scared people trying to escape looked like. I saw it back in Lycaon's city-state. People were going to get seriously hurt if something wasn't done.

Where the hell were the security guards? Shouldn't they be stopping this?

Then I remembered that the last vandalism attack

at this temple may have been an inside job. Someone on the security detail here had a problem with the Gods.

"We need to do something," I told Jia. "We need to keep our true selves under cover, but that doesn't mean we can't shut these guys down."

"You take those; I'll take the others," she replied, and even before I moved toward the closest thugs, Jia turned and went after the other two in the far side of the temple.

When they saw me coming, one of them fired a few shots at my chest, probably thinking I would be deterred and wouldn't want to get involved in whatever it was they were doing. Of course, he'd be wrong on that point. I very much wanted to get involved.

"Stop right there, Son. You don't want to get hurt," the one who shot at me warned. He looked like he was in his forties, with a bit of a beer gut and a scruff on his face. His appearance was that of an average guy, who probably worked some labor-intensive job, was married and had kids. On any other day, I'd imagine him to be a good man, but today he was a problem—drunk on the feeling of belonging to a group of people smarter than everyone else.

"I'm not your son. Why are you doing this?" I asked, moving even closer to him.

He wouldn't be able to hurt me, not with some stupid paint gun. He had probably fifty pounds on me, and a couple of inches in height, but he still wouldn't be a match for me in hand-to-hand combat. Little did he know, I was the one who had to consider how not to hurt him if it came down to a fight.

"The Gods have been lying and manipulating us for years. It's time they are toppled from their altars." To prove his point, I guessed, he took aim at Zeus's statue and fired five shots onto the alabaster stone. Red explosions stained Zeus's pristine form, from his head down to his gut.

The urge to inform the man that Zeus no longer existed coursed through me, but I had to tamp it down. This uprising—I figured this was as good a confirmation as we were going to get—was about all the Gods and not just Zeus. There was no point on telling him. Firstly, I didn't think it would matter to him, and secondly, I needed to find out more about what he and the others were trying to do, and how they were going to proceed. This didn't feel like an isolated incident.

"That may be true," I conceded, trying to placate him first, "but what you're doing to these innocent people isn't helping."

"They aren't innocent. They're helping the Gods by

coming here and making their stupid offers. That's how the Gods gain their power."

The way he licked his lips, his gaze never meeting mine, told me he was nervous. It made me wonder if he even truly meant what he was saying. There was some doubt there. Maybe it was enough for me to play on, and get more information.

Before I could get the chance though, his buddy came at me from the right, jamming the barrel of his air rifle into my side. "Back the fuck up man, or I will hurt you."

I took that moment to do a quick check over my shoulder to see where Jia was and how she was faring. The temple interior was pretty much empty, save for me, the two men I was dealing with, and Jia, who was slowly making her way toward me. What she did to the other assailants wasn't clear, but there was no sign of them now. Maybe they had run.

"Can't do much with this." Gripping the end of his rifle, I shoved him backward. It took him off guard, and he didn't like that. He didn't appreciate the obvious strength he felt in my light shove, either.

His face reddened, and he lifted his black military shirt to reveal a blade fastened to his belt. "I'll give you a second chance, boy. But you won't get a third."

"Steve, what the hell?" the other thug sputtered at his partner. "Mark told us not to bring real weapons…"

"Shut up!" his partner shouted, his face getting redder by the second. Setting one hand on the hilt of his knife, but before he could pull it out, Jia came charging from behind him—she was really quick, probably faster than either men had ever seen. Her hands gripped his shoulders, and she flipped him onto his back. He didn't stand a chance once she pressed her foot onto his neck, effectively cutting off his air supply.

I gave her a warning look, and she lessened the pressure not to kill, but just render him unconscious. Jia shrugged at me, unconcerned.

The man I'd been talking to, glanced from her to me. "You're those Demigods. The kids indoctrinated into that academy."

"We're not kids," I rebutted. "And we haven't been brainwashed like you."

Panicking, he turned to make a run for the exit, except I couldn't let him go. He had information we needed, and I didn't think it would take too much to get it out of him.

My wings swiftly unfurled, and I shot toward him, grabbing him under the arms and lifting him into the air.

"Let me go!" he shouted, kicking his feet to get free.

The sounds coming out of his mouth became an inhuman shriek when I flew him higher, until we hovered above the statue of Zeus.

If I dropped him now, he'd definitely break something. To be honest, I was irritated with his little display of false power, so I wasn't sure I cared anymore. Thankfully for him, he quickly realized that, and stopped struggling.

Below us, Jia nudged the guy on the ground with her shoe, none too gently. "What should we do with him?"

"We could Scooby Doo him and tie him up to leave for the police." I grinned down at her when the man sputtered in my grasp.

She chuckled. "I like that. Scooby Doo him."

The sound of sirens filled the hall, telling me we were too late to tie him up. Damn. I'd always wanted to do that Scooby Doo thing.

"Leave him."

She did.

"Can you play a victim? Stay and tell the police everything that happened?"

After nodding, she rolled her shoulders to make sure her wings were tucked in all the way. "What are you going to do?"

"Take this guy out somewhere to ask him some questions. He has answers we need."

"Okay. Go. I'll see you back at the apartment."

Flying higher, I went out through the opening in the roof. All temples had those skylights, so that the Gods could send down their blessings. Thankfully, no one was looking up, all their attention was on the ground, on the vandalised shrine and those who had been attacked, so I carried the guy over the buildings.

"You might as well drop me, I'm not going to tell you anything," he challenged, his voice a bit shaky while I flew us across town and out toward an abandoned field. It looked like the same one where the others and I battled Lycaon's undead army. I couldn't fly all the way back to the apartment. It would draw too much attention, so this had to do.

The moment we touched down, he made a run for it through the tall grass. I lifted back into the air, then landed in front of him. "You can't outrun me. I can fly faster than a car can drive."

Not listening to me, he tried again. Shaking my head, I shot up into the air like a bullet and came right back down the same way, landing a mere few feet in front of him. He had to put on the brakes or plow right into me. The momentum sent him sprawling, and he crashed on his knees on the dirt.

Before he could scramble back to his feet, which I could tell was his intention, I extended a hand toward the grass surrounding us. Flames instantly shot out, growing tall as they whipped around in a complete circle, until we were enclosed inside a ring of fire.

His eyes bugged out, and his breath becoming hard and fast. The fear was clear on his face. Everyone was afraid of fire.

Giving up, he sat down and closed his eyes. "What do you want from me?"

"What was the purpose of your actions today?"

He shrugged. "To scare people, I guess."

"To stop them from coming to the temple?"

He nodded. "Yeah."

"Okay, then what? What was the next move? Because I know this is about more than a few temples around the area."

"I don't know. I'm not privy to that information."

"What's the main goal? Why did you sign up for this?"

His hand rubbed the stubble on his chin before his head hung. "To stop the recruitment of our children." When he lifted his head again, his gaze bore into mine. "To stop my kids and all the others from becoming something like you."

CHAPTER THIRTEEN

NICOLE

"*I*'m pretty sure we're going to have to run."

There was another shimmer and vibration of the air around Cerberus, like he was somehow fighting my time hold, or this place was. Maybe it was just me. The time freezing wasn't going to last much longer, and I hated that I didn't have complete control over it by now.

Turning all the way around, Cassandra pointed toward the dark gaping maw of a cave behind us. It looked like a mouth, with sharp daggers of rock for teeth. "That way."

I sprinted toward the entrance while Cassandra followed my lead. Tinker swiftly came with us and we entered the belly of the stone beast. The cave was even darker than the world outside it, so I created another ball of fire, tossing it ahead of us to light our way. The orange glow flickered along the craggy cave walls, as we ran toward what I assumed would be the door to Hades's Hall.

It wasn't long before I heard the sputtering rush of the great river. Time had restarted. Three loud growls came from the same direction, soon turning into mewls. The giant hound was probably confused as to where we had gone. It wouldn't take long before he figured out that we'd tricked him, crossed the river, and we were now on the way to the door.

The muscles in my legs strained when I picked up my pace. I knew I'd have a few aches and pains when this was all over and we were back at the academy, even though running was my specialty. Nothing one of Chiron's healing salves wouldn't take care of though, so I pushed even harder.

The light from my orange fire ball was waning, so I made another one and tossed it ahead of us again. This time it hit something. Something hard and metallic by the sound of it; sparks spread out of it. It had to be the door. We were almost there, but what if we knocked and no one answered? I hadn't considered that before now.

"Are you sure Hecate is down here?" I was ever so slightly winded, which was saying something.

"I'm positive." Cassandra's hand strayed to her daggers again as she ran.

The doors became visible for the first time, looming in the near distance—and as black as the rocks surrounding them. Relief surged through me at seeing them, but it was quickly cut off when a thunderous bark echoed through the cave. Cerberus was hot on our heels.

I increased the speed for the last few feet, and the second I reached the doors, I started banging on them. "Hello! We need to speak to Hecate!"

Cassandra also knocked on it. "It's Cassandra, please let us in!"

Another bark and growl came from the shadows behind us, and I swore I could almost feel the hound's breath on the back of my neck. The stench of it invaded my nose with rotting meat, brimstone, and thousands of years of skipped tooth brushing was overwhelming. I nearly retched. Cerberus would soon be upon us, and I wasn't sure if I could stop time a second time.

Thankfully, a loud clank reverberated, then the

metal doors swung open. A skeletal figure in a black hood stood in the entranceway. It was Charon.

"I'm Cassandra." She took a step forward, voice urgent. "I was a friend of Melany's. Do you remember?"

"I know you." His raspy voice confirmed before his hooded skull slowly turned toward me. "I do not know you."

"My name's Nicole…" Another growl echoed through the cave, making me flinch. "I'm sure we can get to know each other better inside." I took a step forward, but his bony fingers came up and I bounced up against an invisible shield, hitting my nose rather harshly.

"Bloody hell." I rubbed at it, tears welling in my eyes from the sharp pain. "What is it about the nose?"

Tinker pressed against my leg, a series of concerned bleeps and bloops bursting out of him.

Charon's skull dropped down toward the little robot, the sounds catching his attention. "What is that?"

"That's Tinker. I made him." I placed a hand on the little guy's head protectively, but Charon seemed genuinely curious rather than predatory.

"We have a serving robot here, but not like that one." The interest was strong in his raspy, harsh words.

"I'll make you one just like him, if you let us in." A promise I could keep, but only if I was alive to do it.

"You may enter," he finally conceded, still looking at Tinker—much the way a person couldn't look away from an incredibly cute puppy.

Cautious that I wasn't going to smack my face against something again, I slowly took a step forward, leading with my shoulder instead of my throbbing nose. Nothing impeded my advance, and I was able to fully walk into the hall. Cassandra came right after, followed by Tinker, who rolled up from behind me, staying very close to my side. I was thankful for that; I needed his comfort as much as he needed mine.

I whipped around just as Cerberus's three large heads came into view—mouths open, and his rotten green saliva dripping from between long jagged fangs. With a wave of Charon's hand, the doors swung shut right before the beast could come bursting into the hall.

A thunderous thud sounded against the metal doors, but right after, three very pitiful whines echoed. Cerberus was not an incredibly cute puppy, and I wanted to get the hell away from him.

Panting hard, I braced a hand against the marble wall to catch my breath. Also, to calm my heart, which still thudded like a hammer against my ribs. After being around Gods and Demigods, and strange beasts for years, you'd think nothing else could scare me. Well, that would be so very wrong. Cerberus was bloody frightening.

To think that Melany had tamed that beast, riding him into battle like a valiant stead boggled my mind.

As I tried to regain my composure, I took that reprieve to survey the hall. Cassandra had been right about it being opulent. The black-and-white tiles gleamed under my feet, as if they were made of glass. Soft orange light emanated from the walls, where flames flickered from a foot wide slit near the bottom of the wall. There was no furniture in the foyer, nothing to welcome visitors, which I found very cold and bleak despite the warm fire light.

I supposed one person's palace was another's prison.

"Now," Charon rasped, the sound strange coming from bones with no flesh covering them, "what do you want?"

"We wish to speak with Hecate," I replied, pushing away from the wall, finally feeling a little less unnerved and off balance.

"Why do you wish to speak to—"

"Charon, I can speak for myself."

Just past the skeletal man, was a darkly ethereal woman with long black hair and pale skin, standing in the middle of the hall. She was dressed in a form-fitting black dress that pooled around her on the floor, so long that I didn't see how she could walk, but maybe the answer was that she just didn't. I hadn't seen where she came from, she was just suddenly there.

"Fetch us some tea," she said to him. "We'll take in the library."

With a curt nod, Charon literally floated away. A door along one wall opened for him, and he disappeared through it.

She gestured toward an open doorway at the very end of the hall, on the right. Politely, she waited for us to enter, then followed us. As I passed her, I had the distinct sense that she glowered at me, although her face had been turned away. A shiver rushed down my back at the sensation. Weird.

"Please, sit." Her hand motioned toward the ornate, velvet covered chairs around the large fireplace at the end of the room. A fire had been lit. It crackled and snapped when I settled into the nearest chair.

Once we were all seated, Charon appeared with a tray that held a prettily painted, and delicate tea pot with three cups. While he poured the hot brown liquid into a cup, and handed it to me, pangs of missing home stabbed me in the belly.

"Milk?" he asked, his voice as crumbly as the ash

in the fireplace. Nodding, I watched him pour a small amount into my cup, then handed me a spoon. It was all very polite and civilized. It was very strange to think I was sitting in Hades's old library, having tea with a powerful witch, and being served by a skeleton.

I sipped the tea, sighing with how good it tasted. I hadn't been able to get a good cuppa since leaving London. "Oh, that's nice. Thank you."

Hecate stared at me over the rim of her cup as she drank. "Who are you?"

"I'm Nicole Walker. I used to be at the academy years ago, before Zeus ripped out my memories and abandoned me on the streets of London." I was surprised that I had blurted out all that. Obviously, I was still bitter and dealing with the trauma. Who knew?

A knowing gleam entered her eyes; she nodded. "You're the girl who can move through time."

"Yes."

"What can I help you with?"

My attention shifted to Cassandra, hoping she could jump in since she knew the witch and the God of Sleep while I didn't. "We were hoping to speak with Hypnos."

"Why?" Hecate's voice hardened a little. Before, it

had been sort of musical, but now it sounded harsh and cold.

"I need to ask him about Melany," I admitted.

Her brow furrowed. "Melany? She's gone."

"I know, but…" I wasn't sure what to divulge about what was happening to me. I had only told Cassandra and Cade, so I didn't want to tell someone I didn't even know or trust.

"You don't believe she's really gone," the witch concluded.

I scrunched up my face. "Well, I didn't say that."

"You're not the first person to come asking." Hecate set her teacup down, her head tilting to eye Cassandra. "Lucian was down here a few times too, looking for answers."

Well, that was cruel. Something told me Hecate was a bit of a bitch and got off on it.

"I know," Cassandra casually replied. "He told me. We don't keep secrets from each other."

A snide smile curved Hecate's lips. "How refreshing."

I cleared my throat. "Can we speak with Hypnos or not?"

"Of course, but you'll have to stay the night. Hypnos will only speak to you in your dreams. I've had

Charon already make up the guest rooms for you." She stood. "I'll see you in the morning."

I frowned. "But it's not night, and I'm not tired."

That snide smile returned as she folded her hands primly at her waist. "Aren't you?"

Then it hit me like a tidal wave. I yawned, barely able to keep my eyes open. It was hard to remember a time when I'd been so tired in my life. Realization floated over me, and I glanced down at the tea in the cup I was still holding. She had drugged us.

I looked over at Cassandra, seeing she'd dropped her cup onto the floor, the last bit of her tea spilling out onto the fur rug.

"Charon, will show you to your rooms."

Like magic, the hooded butler appeared in front of us. Of course, I knew it wasn't exactly magic, but likely that he traveled through the shadows, like all of the dark-leaning Gods and Demigods did. Despite my urge to fight back, I got to my feet, following him out of the library and down the hall without complaint. A floaty feeling captured me whole until I just wanted to lie down on something soft and close my eyes.

Charon opened a door for me and I went inside. The bedroom was huge and done in rich, deep tones of red, black, and burgundy. The bed was large with a four-poster canopy. It looked like a princess's bed. As I laid down on the thick, pillowy mattress, I realized that this had been Melany's room. Even though I'd never known her, I could feel her presence nonetheless.

After a big stretch, I pulled the soft blanket up over my body, and closed my eyes. It was mere seconds before I fell asleep and went tumbling into a sea of darkness.

CHAPTER FOURTEEN

CADE

*H*atred spilled from the man's eyes as he glared at me, but I also heard the slight reservation in his voice when he spoke. He wasn't one hundred percent on board with their mission or line of reasoning. There was doubt there, and that was something I could hopefully exploit.

I folded in my wings, so I didn't appear so imposing to him. "I didn't become a Demigod just by being at the academy. They don't 'make' you into one. You can't be indoctrinated. A person has to have Gods' blood in them to start with, to even receive a Shadowbox on their birthday."

"Shadowboxes are sent to children whose families give the most to the temples." His voice wavered, clearly questioning it.

"That's not true at all. My family didn't worship much to the Gods. Maybe during one of the special celebrations, or solstices. I never really believed in the Gods myself, and I got my Shadowbox on my eighteenth birthday." I paused for a moment, gauging his expression. "Also, by your logic, all your children would be safe from being chosen. Since you hate the Gods so much, I'm assuming you never give them any offerings. So there you go, all fixed."

He glared at me some more but didn't respond. I supposed it was wishful thinking that he was actually considering my words.

"You've been told a lot of lies," the man finally retorted with a shake of his head, and I felt a surge of frustration.

How could he not see what was so clearly right in front of him?

"Evidently, so have you."

Sighing, he scrubbed his chin again, and looked around at the ring of fire. "Are you going to kill me?"

His blunt question took me off guard, and I made a face. "No. Of course I'm not going to kill you."

"Then, what?" Slowly, he got to his feet. "Keep me in this field forever."

"I will let you go, but only if you tell me who is behind these attacks, and what the end goal is." I tried to keep my voice leveled, non-threatening.

Pinching the bridge of his nose, he shook his head again. "I told you, I don't know the end goal. I'm not in the inner circle."

I didn't think he realized how much information he was giving me. Thanks to him, I now knew that these attacks were organized by a small group, and there was a hierarchy. A hierarchy indicated there were ranks, which meant there was some semblance of an army. Or at least, the beginnings of one.

Slowly, I raised my hand toward the flames and snuffed them. I needed to show some good faith to this guy. Maybe get him to trust that I would stay true to my word and let him go, if he gave me the information I needed.

"I heard you say the name Mark while in the temple. Is that who's calling the shots? Do you have a last name for him?"

He flinched when I mentioned Mark. Obviously, he was someone in charge. The main man in their operation? That I didn't know, but it was at least some kind of lead to follow.

"I'm not going to say anything else." His chin jutted out stubbornly.

"What's your name?" I made a point of looking him in the eye.

For a long moment, he just looked at me, but didn't answer.

"I'm Cade." I offered him my hand.

He still didn't say anything, and certainly didn't shake my hand, but at least he didn't sneer at it or spit on me.

"There's no reason we need to be enemies. I don't always agree with what the Gods do or don't do. They aren't all honest and noble. I know that from experience." Briefly, I toyed with the notion of telling him about Zeus's demise as well as Aphrodite's and Ares's. Maybe if he knew that the worst of them were gone...

"My name is Tom."

"Good to know you, Tom."

After a brief hesitation, he did take my hand that time.

"I want you to know that you can walk away right now and go back to your family. You haven't gone too far, just some vandalism and foolish paintball prank. It doesn't have to go any further for you."

The change in his expression told me he was considering my words. Maybe he was thinking about his family. I hoped he was. Maybe we could end this without any more trouble.

"I do want you to know though, Tom, that if you decide after leaving here today that you are going to continue to be involved with whatever is brewing, you'll be putting innocent people at risk. The danger is real. You may be building an army, and maybe you have some good numbers, but it won't be enough. We are Demigods. We have been training for years to fight these battles. And our weapons aren't only swords and spears…"

Unsheathing the dagger at my belt, I spun it around on the back of my hand, flipping it between my fingers so fast that it became a blur.

"We wield fire, water, earth, rock, steel, and the shadows themselves. We were trained to fight Titans as big as mountains; an army of mortals is inconsequential."

His swallow was audible, and he licked his lips. "Then why are you here? Why are you bothering with me if I'm not a threat? And why should I trust that you care about us any more than we humans care about bugs, if we're so inconsequential?"

"Because we, Demigods, are still part human. Our families and the people we love are here. I don't want to see you, any of you, get hurt. We train at the academy to protect this world from all threats, and that includes protecting them from you and your misguided army."

Dread flickered in his eyes as he shook his head, running a hand through his hair. I was getting to him. He was listening. "Shit. I hate this. Carmen told me to stay out of it."

"Is Carmen your wife?"

He nodded.

"Then listen to her." In all honesty, I didn't think there was anything else I could say to the guy. I just hoped it was enough for him to change his mind about what he was getting involved in before it was too late. "I can fly you back to town…"

"No, I'll walk if its all the same to you." He almost shouted it, and it took everything I had to hold back my grin. I loved flying, loved being in the air, spreading my wings, but clearly Tom hadn't been too keen on his little taste of it—when I dangled him in the air over the statue of Zeus.

"Yup, suit yourself."

Just as Tom gave me a curt nod, and turned to start walking back to town, the sound of a revving engine filled the field. I spun around to see an SUV barrelling across the tall grass toward us. I suspected it was probably full of Tom's buddies. Someone must've seen me lift him out of the temple and they tracked us here.

Tom cursed, then started to run. Away from it, not toward it. That told me those in the SUV might not be as willing to listen to reason as my friend here had, and they might be armed with more than paintball guns.

My wings spread out, and I rose into the air. Tom hadn't gotten too far, so I swooped toward him, picking him up under his arms again. His instinct was to struggle.

"Don't move. I can get us out of here quicker than they can drive."

When he stopped squirming, to let me do my thing, I shot higher into the sky. The extra weight of carrying someone caused some drag, so I wasn't as fast as I could've been. Before I could course correct and get us out of there, the window on the passenger side rolled down and the barrel of a rifle poke out.

At first, I thought they were going to shoot us with more paint pellets, which would be annoying as hell but an inconvenience at most, but the sound the rifle made —a thunderous echoing pop—shook me to the core. It wasn't a paint pellet what pierced Tom's gut and exploded out his back.

They had shot one of their own. Shot him clean through, to get to me. Like he was entirely disposable, or he wasn't a being in his own right. The warm spray of blood and gore that splattered onto my pants made my stomach roil. I had to fight back the urge to retch as Tom sagged in my hands. Looking down, I saw the crimson trail he was leaving as I flew him, us, across the field and away from the SUV as quickly as I could.

Another ringing shot came from the vehicle and I felt the bullet whizz by me, just missing my arm. I veered to the left, hoping they couldn't steer the SUV that fast. Despite my strength, carrying Tom was getting harder and harder by the second. I wasn't sure if I could make it back to town with him. I had to try though, maybe he wasn't dead. Maybe Georgina could heal him.

I risked a peek over my shoulder to see where the vehicle was, and that was a huge mistake.

I felt the bullet before I heard it.

At first, it was like getting punched in the flank with a large mallet, then a rush of heat shot up my spine and the pain set in. A bone deep throb that pulsed in time with every beat of my heart. I knew it was because of the blood rushing out of me.

I couldn't hold onto Tom any longer. I didn't have the strength to carry him and to fly. Not now that I'd been shot. Blood loss was making my head swim. Soon, my eyesight would fade, and I wouldn't be able to stay airborne. Time was ticking, I needed to get back to town and find Georgina so could heal me.

I tried to find a better hold on him, but every second in the air was more energy spent. Slowly, I was descending toward the ground. Soon, I wouldn't be able to flap my right wing. If I wanted to live and see Nicole again, I had to make a decision immediately.

"I'm sorry," I murmured, then released my grip on Tom.

While his body fell to the ground, I was able to fly up higher, away from the SUV and out of range from another bullet. The vehicle came to a stop near Tom's body. All doors opened, and four men dressed in black jumped out of it. Part of me wondered if one of those men was named Mark.

As I flew, I clamped a hand over my wound, hoping to stem the blood. It didn't really work, as it continued soaking the waistband of my pants. The tops of buildings suddenly became visible, downtown Pecunia, so I started to descend. The last thing I wanted was for a bunch of people to see a flying Demigod overhead dripping blood all over their heads.

I dropped down and landed behind some buildings that I recognized were about two blocks from where we were staying. Folding my wings, I started walking toward the apartment. Every so often, I had to stop, leaning up against a wall to catch my breath. Sweat slicked my face and body, and I was seeing black spots in my eyes.

Thankfully, I reached our building and climbed the stairs to the apartment door. When I got to the top, I was out of breath, dizzy. I fell against the door, not enough strength left in me to even turn the knob. Mercifully, the door opened, and I collapsed onto Georgina's feet. I blinked up at her and winced.

"I've been shot... I think I'm dying."

Those were my last words before I passed out cold.

CHAPTER FIFTEEN

NICOLE

*O*nce again, I stood in the time garden—or at least, that's what I called the beautiful, lush garden, with the sun dial that Cade and I had constructed, and he had installed with Hephaistos. It had been my happy place after I returned to the academy. The place where I could find peace and solace. Where I could just be myself, and not have so many people judging me for what I could and couldn't do, could and couldn't be. It was here that Cade and I started hanging out together...

And where I started to fall in love with him.

So, it wasn't a big surprise to find myself there,

thinking about him. Missing him, although we'd only been apart for a few hours.

A few hours? That didn't feel right. It felt both longer and shorter. I guessed that was what it felt like when you were in a dream.

I walked along the cobblestone path, illuminated by the pale light of the full moon, while trailing my fingers over the tips of the tall grass that grew there. Its white, moon flowers grew with abandon, and they always smelled so sweet as they bloomed in the moonlight, so I bent over to sniff one of them. Content, I continued toward the large, stone sundial, and the wooden bench nearby.

Feeling very much at peace, I slid onto the bench and smiled. This was a great dream. I hadn't experienced one so nice in a long time. They had mostly been rehashes of jumping through time, and weird quick flashes of Melany. While I sat there, thinking about how beautiful it was and how much I wished Cade had joined me, a rustling in the trees drew my attention.

I looked up to the treetops, to see a large shape fly off one branch. Was it an owl? There were some really big brown ones that lived in the surrounding woods.

Suddenly, it swooped down toward me, and I realized it wasn't an owl, but some kind of bat. I'd never seen a bat with gray, mottled skin—they usually had fur, black or brown. The bat landed on the sundial. As it perched there—looking much like a gargoyle—it turned its head, focusing glowing red eyes on me. Glancing at it closely, I was pretty sure that creature was not a bat. It looked like a tiny demon.

When it squawked at me, flapping leathery wings as if to warn me, I thought for sure it was going to attack me.

"Please, excuse my little buddy, here. He's a bit cranky." Beside me, emerged a tall, slim figure in a black cloak. He pointed to the bench. "May I sit with you?"

"Um, sure." Frowning, I slid over to make room for him.

"Thanks." He gathered his robe around his body, then sat. Reaching inside his pocket, the figure pulled out a joint, and put it in his mouth—or at least where his mouth should have been, since there was just pitch blackness inside his hood. "Do you mind if I smoke?"

Too stunned to give him a verbal response, I shook my head. What the bloody hell was going on? Who was this guy who showed up in my dream, uninvited?

Lifting one finger, which was as dark as the night surrounding us, the tip produced one tiny flame, and he lit the joint. Curls of gray smoke snaked out from under his hood. The stink of weed instantly filled my nose.

After taking a long draw of it, he offered it to me. "Want a hit?"

"No, I'm good. Thanks."

He took another long hit, then crossed his legs, revealing he was wearing flip flops on his pitch black feet. "So, what did you want to talk to me about?"

Eyes widening, I turned to gape at him. Now I remembered why I was there. I was in the Underworld, had tea with Hecate, and she'd drugged me so I could go to sleep and meet with…

"You're Hypnos?"

The obscure figure nodded. "Yup. I know, I'm a bit of a surprise to everyone. What do you think the God of Sleep and Dreams should look like? Like Apollo, with golden hair and chiseled abs?" He snickered. "This is not that type of dream, if you know what I mean." Chuckling to himself, Hypnos took another hit on the joint.

To be honest, I didn't really know what to expect. However, it certainly wasn't some hooded "bro", who sounded like he'd be more at home on a surfboard, riding the Californian waves, than tending to one of my dreams.

"But if *that* kind of dream is what you're really here

for, I could summon good old Cade." His head tilted to the side, as if he was in deep thought. "Nah, I don't think he'd be up for it. He's having a bit of an issue right now."

Panicked, I grabbed his arm and squeezed. "What do you mean he's having an issue? Did something happen to him?"

"Whoa, you're way stronger than you look." Hypnos pried my hand away from his arm.

"Is Cade hurt?"

"You didn't come to see me to talk about Cade. What did you want to talk to me about?"

All of a sudden, I began feeling muddled, so I shook my head to clear it. It felt like someone was stirring my thoughts and feelings around with a large wooden spoon.

I rubbed at my forehead, trying to regain focus. "Um, I… want to know, um, about…" Think, Nicole! My eyes closed, and the second they did, an image flashed behind my lids. A girl with blue hair and lightning scars. I snapped them open again. "Melany! I came to ask you about Melany."

Hypnos's hood turned toward me, suggesting he was looking at me. Despite the fact that he had no face and therefore no eyes, it felt like it. "What do you want to know?"

"Is she truly dead?"

"Why do you need to know?"

"Because I keep seeing her. And twice now I've accidentally opened a portal to… well, I have no idea where she is, but I see her, and I can talk to her." A heavy sigh left me, and I leaned back against the bench. "If she's dead, then I'm opening portals to the afterlife, and that's pretty much effed up, mate. I don't know how to deal with that, or what to do about it. After fighting Lycaon and his zombie army, I'm pretty much done dealing with the dead."

His back rested against the bench, and he sighed too, stretching out his legs. Hypnos took one last pull off the joint, then put it out with his fingers. Before he could say anything though, a cold gust of wind blew at us, fluttering the bottom of his robe and my hair.

From the dark shadows, another hooded figure stepped into a swatch of pale moonlight. He was Hypnos's twin. "Do not dare speak of it, Brother," the man commanded, his voice as old as weathered papyrus that cracked when handled.

"Dude, chill. I wasn't going to say anything."

Pulse racing, I jumped to my feet. "Holy shit. You're Death."

"I am. And you are Nicole Walker. We have almost met a couple of times over the past year."

My heart sunk into my stomach at that statement, to know that I had almost died. Like for real. I mean, I was in a bad state when I jumped Cassandra, the Corpse King, and myself to the Jurassic era and my arm was infected from the zombie's touch… and of course, I could never forget almost disintegrating in the wheel of time, but both times turned out okay and I survived. It was freaky to know that I was that close to actual death. For some that might have been liberating, but for me, that scared the stuffing out of me.

Hands fluttering about, I paced back and forth in front of the bench. "What are you doing here? Am I going to die in my sleep? Did Hecate give me too much of her sleeping potion?! Shit. I don't want to die. I've got too much to do still."

Obviously, I was panicking, but I couldn't stop. I wouldn't get a chance to say goodbye to Cade. That wasn't fair. After all I'd done for the academy, for the whole world actually, this couldn't be how it would all end.

"No. I am not here to take your soul, Nicole."

"Yeah. So, chill, dude." Hypnos tried to give me the rest of his weed. "Maybe you should take this. I think you need it more than I do."

Halting my steps, I stared at Thanatos. "Then why are you in my dream?"

"To stop my brother from breaking a promise we made to Melany."

Hypnos threw his hands in the air. "I wasn't going to say anything. Man, you're not the trusting sort."

"So, she's not dead."

"I did not say that."

"But you did NOT not say that. I think if she was just run of the mill dead, you wouldn't be going to all these lengths to stop me from finding out. You'd be like, 'yeah, she's dead. Deal with it.'"

Thanatos glared at me, or at least I assumed it was a glare. I couldn't tell, because he had no face, just like Hypnos, but I felt a really intense energy coming out from the darkness under his hood. Something told me he was thinking about maybe reneging that "I didn't come here to kill you" thing he'd just said.

His hooded face turned to Hypnos. "Can you do something about her, Brother? She is giving me a raging headache."

"But you didn't answer my questions!" I felt like stomping my foot and having a real go at a temper tantrum.

Both he and Hypnos shrugged. Then the Dream God stood, reached over, and tapped me right between the eyes. "Wake up."

Before I was fully jolted out of the dream, Thanatos's voice made my heart jump into my throat.

"I have got to get back. I think her boyfriend is about to—"

I sat up in the bed, heartbeats thundering in my ears. Sweat slicked my entire body, and my hands shook violently. Cade! Something had happened to him.

Jumping off the bed, I marched toward the door and went out into the hall. "Cassandra!"

I didn't know which room she was in, so my first thought was to scream her name until she emerged from behind one of the closed doors.

"Cassandra! Where are you?" Running to the next room, I opened the door. It was a dining room with a long wooden table and six ornate chairs tucked in under it, but it was empty.

Another door opened along the far wall and Charon floated out from it. "What is the matter?"

Behind him, to my surprise, wheeled Tinker. He was carrying a tray of what looked like champagne flutes, and he was wearing a server's uniform that consisted of a white top and black skirt. A blond wig with pretty, blond curls sat on top of his dome head. He looked like a robot version of Shirley Temple.

"Um," I gaped at the little robot and at Charon. "Do I even want to ask?"

Tinker dropped the tray, proceeding to make a

series of wild beeps and bloops. "It is not what it looks like, Nicole. Charon and I were just playing around."

Shaking my head, I just left the room, in search of Cassandra. We needed to get the hell out of there.

"Cassandra!" I bellowed as loud as I could.

Right then, Hecate came out of the library, holding a champagne flute. "Why are you shouting in my hall?"

Another set of doors opened, and Cassandra came running out. She must've been sleeping like I had been, drugged by Hecate's tea, because her hair was in disarray and her clothes were askew. She rubbed at her eyes. "What's going on?"

Rushing to her, I grabbed her hands. "Cade's in trouble. I think he's going to die."

CHAPTER SIXTEEN

CADE

*A*s I lay on the ground, immobile, I had a sense that someone was standing over me, looking down into my face, studying me. However, I couldn't really see anyone, it was just a shapeless form. A solid piece of darkness. I knew if I had been able to lift my hand and reach out, I would touch something made out of flesh and blood. The someone had a name, I was sure of it. It swirled around in my mind, but I didn't want to utter it out loud. Only bad luck came of doing such a thing.

Bad luck. That was what I seemed to be hip deep inside of right now. And it hurt. Like, badly, right in my side. No, wait. That hadn't been bad luck. That had been a… bullet? Yes. That seemed right. I had been shot while trying to fly an injured man back to the apartment.

The form above me moved. *"Good. You are going back to where you belong. It is not quite time for us to meet, Cade."*

Going back where?

"Nicole will be pleased to know you are not—"

"Cade?" A tap on my cheek brought me back.

"Wait! Nicole? What about Nicole?" I screamed into the void.

Everything was still blank, with a dark outline, but I could "see" something behind my eyes—movement, shapes. Sounds filled my ears. Smells filtered into my nose. Straining hard, I cracked open one eyelid, then the other, until I was blinking back tears from the harsh light beaming into my eyes from a window nearby.

"Someone close the curtains."

A few moments later, the light was muted, and I was able to glance around, actually making out things surrounding me. I was in a bedroom, that much was clear, laying on a soft mattress while Georgina and Jia looked down on me with concerned pinches to their faces.

"Thank the Gods." Georgina sighed. "I didn't know if you were going to make it."

"What—?" My throat was too dry, making it hard to speak.

Instantly noticing the problem, Georgina offered me some water. She held my head as I sat up a little to drink. It hurt, especially my right side, from just moving that small amount.

"That's what we need to be asking you," Marek said as he moved into my viewpoint. "What happened?"

"Where's… Tom?"

They all frowned, exchanging a glance. "Who's Tom? Was it the guy you lifted out of the temple?" Jia asked.

I nodded.

"You were alone, Cade. You collapsed against the door." Georgina shook her head. "I'm surprised you were even able to make it back with the amount of blood you lost."

"How long?"

"You've been out for about four hours."

My gaze drifted to the bedroom door when Lucian and Jasmine entered.

"Good, you're awake." Lucian gave me a small smile. "I thought we were going to have to take you back to the academy."

In a body bag. Was the unspoken last part of that sentence.

Jia got up from the chair beside the bed for Lucian to sit. He pulled it up closer. "Are you able to tell us everything now?"

Nodding, I licked my lips. Georgina gave me another drink of water before I started talking. I told them everything that Tom had revealed, and about how we were ambushed in the field by four men in an SUV. My teeth gritted in anger and shame when I recalled having to drop Tom so I could escape—I told them, nonetheless.

Lucian's hand patted my knee through the blanket. "You did the only thing you could do, Cade. That guy chose his fate when he signed up with this group."

Logic said that was likely true, so I nodded. However, I sensed that after our conversation, Tom would've thought twice about what he was doing with those people, and hopefully quit. I didn't know for sure, but in my heart, I believed that was a possibility. Now his kids were going to grow up without a father, and I suspected those men would use his death to help radicalize his wife and family. It wouldn't surprise me if those thugs told them that I had been the one to kill Tom, and not them.

"It's obvious this is very much about the academy

and not just the Gods." Frowning, Lucian leaned back in the chair.

"Maybe someone's mad they didn't get their Shadowbox?" Jasmine suggested. "This seems about revenge or pay back."

"Maybe..." Lucian didn't appear convinced.

I thought about what Tom said about his kids and what the academy had "done" to me, turning me into what he considered a freak, I imagined. Something dangerous. Something corruptive.

"It's about us," I concluded. "About the kids who go to the academy."

Recognition colored his expression, and Lucian nodded. "Yeah, makes sense. The men you encountered at the temple were middle-aged, right? In their late forties maybe?"

"Around there, I'd say," Jia answered. "The two I dealt with had patches of gray hair, soft bellies. Definitely had 'Dad' energy."

"So, parents whose kids didn't get into the academy?" Jasmine offered, not convinced.

"Or those of kids who did," I considered, trying to sit up.

Georgina glared at me. "I hope you aren't trying to get out of that bed."

"I just need to sit up. I'm feeling better, I promise."

Lies. Of course I didn't feel better, but I didn't want to appear weak and useless, not any more than I already did. It wasn't my fault that I got shot, I knew that, yet I still had some guilt clinging to my chest.

It was clear that Georgina didn't believe me, and still, she helped me to get propped up against the bedframe with a couple of pillows behind my back. Once I was sitting up, I looked down at myself. There was a stretch of bandage wrapped around my stomach. A bit of blood bloomed on my right side, where I'd obviously been shot.

"You shouldn't have moved," she growled. "Now you're bleeding again."

Lucian got up so Georgina could take the chair and fix me up again. She unwrapped the gauze, and I realized the damage a bullet could do. My entire right side was black and blue, bruised by the impact to my muscles. The entrance wound itself was surprisingly small, but I suspected that wasn't how it had looked without Georgina's healing skills.

Blood oozed from where it had pulled open. There weren't any stitches as that was not how we healed. Georgina would've knitted my flesh back together with the power in her hands, and a bit of fire to cauterize the hole. It was actually quite amazing what she could do.

"Thankfully, the bullet came in and out the back, without hitting anything. The back looks worse, but it was easier to knit back together."

As she set her hand over the wound and pushed her power into me, the others watched, and their expressions said it all. There was a mixture of anger and concern, but also, I saw realization there. We had come here with bravado, and the confidence that we were Demigods with unimaginable powers, but maybe we were naïve to think that the mortals wouldn't just come bearing guns or worse bombs. I think the years of training at the academy with everything but firearms, had made us somewhat naïve to the realities of the mortal world.

If the bullet had hit one of my vital organs, or my head, I wouldn't be alive. Not without the immortal power of the Gods themselves.

A hissed breath escaped me when Georgina pushed a bit too hard on my side, but I didn't complain, just endured it. I'd deal with it if it afforded her the chance to heal me fully. When she was done, she wrapped me up in a new bandage and dug into her leather pouch, pulling out a small brown glass ampule.

Uncorking it, she handed it to me. "Drink it. It will numb any pain."

I downed it, grimacing from the taste, but used to it

—I had drunk many similar tinctures given to me by Chiron. The last time being only a few months ago, to heal my busted leg from when an undead soldier struck me with a heavy metal chain.

Lucian looked around at everyone standing in the bedroom. The others were probably waiting in the living room for a plan. "We need to tell Prometheus what's happened. This changes the game, I think."

Everyone nodded in agreement.

"It's too bad these cell phones don't work between realms." Marek pulled out the phone from his pocket. He'd been standing in the corner, near the window, while taking a peek past the curtains to the street every now and then.

"Demeter has a cell phone that works," both Lucian and I blurted out at the same time.

Lucian nodded to Georgina. "You're in her inner circle. Do you know anything about how that works?"

She smirked. "You're kidding yourself if you think I know any of Demeter's secrets. Besides that, she's a Goddess. I'm sure she's not operating off a cell phone tower."

"We could use the lantern," Jasmine suggested, pointing at the brass lantern sitting on the bedside table.

"It's not urgent enough," Lucian countered. "What

if Prometheus's isn't in his office?" He scrubbed at his face and blew out a frustrated breath. "Okay, one of us will go back."

Marek took a step forward. "Why don't we all go back? Clearly, this mission is effed." He gestured to me. "I mean, Cade almost died."

"No." I shook my head. "It's too important that we stay. We can still gather intel. What if the group attacks one of the temples again and this time hurts a bunch of people? I have no doubt that they are just getting started, and that the incident with me and Tom isn't going to deter them. In fact, I have a sense it will spur them on to push their agenda harder and faster."

"I agree with Cade. We can't abandon our mission or the people of Pecunia."

"Okay, so who makes the most sense to return to the academy?" Jasmine asked.

"I'll go," Lucian offered. "I'm too recognizable here, and I'm the most qualified to plan strategy with Prometheus."

Everyone but Marek nodded. He didn't want to be here, that had been obvious from the start, which made me wonder why he'd even come. Surely, he could've told Lucian to pick someone else. Lucian didn't seem the type to force anyone to do something they truly didn't want to do, regardless of the circumstances.

"While I'm gone, Jasmine and Cade are in charge. We need to find out more about this group, who they are recruiting, how they are recruiting and who's in charge. Let's find out who this Mark is. He sounds like the obvious person of interest."

"Let's allow Cade to get some rest." While Georgina gathered her healing supplies and put them back into her leather pouch, the others filed out of the room.

Before Lucian could leave, I called him back. "I need a favor."

"Sure. What is it?"

"Check on Nicole for me. When I was… ah, asleep, I think maybe I had a visit from…"

"Thanatos."

I nodded. "Yeah. And before I… came back, he mentioned her. That tells me that she's either in big trouble, or she's…" I swallowed, not wanting to voice my greatest fear.

He touched my leg. "I'll find her. Try not to think the worst. She's with Cassandra, isn't she?"

"Yeah, I know what they have planned and it isn't a girls' night."

"Cass is level-headed. She won't let Nicole get into any situation she knows they can't get out of."

"Thanks."

He gave me a final squeeze on my leg, then left the room.

I didn't know Cassandra as well as he did, obviously, but I knew Nicole. Even if her plan was reckless, she was going to do it regardless of who was telling her it was a bad idea. I'd instructed Tinker to keep an eye on her during her adventure to the underworld, but I also knew that the little robot was just as in love with her as I was and could be easily persuaded to go along with another one of her crazy plans.

CHAPTER SEVENTEEN

NICOLE

"There has to be a faster way for us to get back to the academy." The urgency to leave was raging like a wildfire in my blood. We had to get back. Something bad was happening or had happened to Cade. Thanatos and Hypnos all but confirmed that in the garden.

"The only other way is through the shadows," Cassandra offered.

I grabbed her hand in desperation. "Can you use the shadows?"

To my dismay, she shook her head. "Not well. It

isn't a power I developed. Only those connected to the darkness can utilize them properly."

"Yeah, I can't use them either." My attention went toward Hecate, who had yet to comment on anything.

She was just standing there, her head cocked, hands folded primly while she watched us with a slight interest. Honestly, she looked like she'd rather go back to the library and read the thick tomes on astrophysics or something as boring.

"Can you take us through the shadows to the academy?"

"No."

I frowned. "No, you can't, or no you won't."

"I'm done helping those from the academy. When Melany promised that I could stay here, she said I'd be left alone. That is what I want. I helped you speak with Hypnos, and that is all I will agree to doing. You are on your own." Turning, she slowly walked back to the library, and shut the door behind her. The sound reverberated through the barren corridor. It was the sound of finality.

"Great." I threw my hands in frustration. "Who else can travel the shadows?"

Suddenly, a loud shriek reverberated around us, followed by a bang, and then a spine-tingling cackling from one of the other closed doors. I glanced at

Cassandra but she just shrugged. Obviously, there were others living in the hall. Other beings who were connected to the dark. Maybe one of them could take us to the academy.

Marching over to the door, I opened it and went inside. Normally, I would've knocked and waited for someone to invite me in, but there wasn't time for being polite right now. It was pitch black in the room, and I couldn't see a thing, but the space felt cavernous. Definitely bigger than it seemed logical. I had to remember that nothing was logical in the Underworld.

A sense of movement reached me, accompanied by the distinct sound of wings flapping. A light, cool breeze brushed over me, making me shiver before little hairs on my arms rose. Lifting my hand, I formed a ball of fire, holding it up in front of me. The warm orange light cascaded across the wooden floor for about ten feet.

I could make out a couple of wooden spears lying on the ground, and a wicked looking dagger with a curved edge. Then I saw what appeared to be a leather whip. Beyond that, there were pale, colored sticks scattered on the wood, but the closer I got to them, I realized that they weren't sticks… they were bones.

Giving me a startle, Cassandra pressed up behind

me. "We should get out of here," she whispered in my ear.

She was right, this had been a bad idea. We would just leave the same way we came. Out the big doors, over the river, across the barren wasteland, and back through the hidden door to the gazebo in the maze. It would take us a lot longer, but at this point, I thought a bit of time was better than eminent death.

Honestly, that was what it felt like in this room. Death. It smelled like it too. My nose wrinkled as the stench invaded my nostrils.

Whipping around, I grabbed Cassandra, and we ran for the open door. It slammed shut right before we got there, plunging us into complete darkness when the flames in my hand snuffed out while in motion. There was scuttling nearby, as if a hundred crabs were moving under foot, heading to the ocean. I swallowed down my rising panic. I needed a level head right now.

Opening my hand, I lit another fire. Once I raised it to light the area near the door, so I could find the handle and turn it, I came face to face with a bat like creature with red hair.

Oh, bloody hell. It was one of the Furies.

"Where are you going?" she hissed.

"Ah, out? It was a mistake coming in here. We're sorry to have disturbed you," I rambled, hoping that my voice didn't quiver. I knew my heart was racing, so I prayed to the Gods that the Furies couldn't hear it. Although, they likely did with those bat-like ears. I'd heard that they responded to fear and terror in the same way that a child responded to a circus with ponies and acrobats. It excited them.

"But we haven't even played a game yet." She leaned in closer to me, smirking. Her razor-sharp kitten teeth were stained red, and there was something stuck in between the front incisors.

My gut roiled over when I realized it was a tiny bit of bloody flesh. She'd obviously just had a meal, and I didn't want to speculate what that was.

"We didn't come to play with you," Cassandra answered.

"No? What did you come for, then?"

"Ah, we were hoping you could take us through the shadows and back to the academy." I didn't know why I told her, asking was absolutely pointless. The Furies were infamous for being manipulative, conniving, and generally awful in all regards. They were definitely not going to help us, unless we had something to barter with. Like our lives.

Mocking laughter burst from behind us. I swung around with my fireball to see the three of them were surrounding us, like this was some sort of game. A game Cassandra and I didn't have a chance at winning.

Since I came back to the academy, I'd heard stories about them. Stories meant to frighten and unnerve. They were like the bogeyman that you looked for under the bed and in your dark closet. It was still hard to believe that Melany had befriended them. They had even fought in the last war at her side, defending the Demigods against Zeus. After Melany's departure, it was obvious they had gone back to their singular malicious ways.

Done playing around, I squeezed Cassandra's hand to let her know, and snapped my fingers.

Just in time too, because when I turned back around, the one with the red hair had been unsheathing the blade at her waist. Another minute, and I suspected that knife would've been plunged into either Cassandra or me without a thought.

"Oh, Gods," Cassandra groaned, realizing the same thing.

"I can't believe Melany dealt with these bitches." I shoved one of them hard, forcing her back and away from us. She tumbled over onto the wooden floor like a mannequin. The tip of her leathery wing bent backwards. I was so not sorry for that.

"I don't think she had a choice, to be honest."

Cassandra helped me move the red head away from the door so we could leave.

Taking the dagger from the Fury's hand, I wrapped my fingers around the blade and fired up my power. The knife melted, leaving it in a puddle at the Furies' feet.

Before we left the room, I went over to the weapons on the floor, plucking a spear from the pile and a dagger, which I tucked into the belt of my jeans. Once we were outfitted—Cassandra had her knives already, just in case we ran into something else or time started again and the Furies came after us—we ran out of the room, heading for the main hall doors.

Thankfully, time was still frozen as we opened the large metal doors and ran out into the cave, because Cerberus had been curled up into a ball near the doors, sleeping. I didn't even want to imagine what would've happened if time had started again. We would've been running right into the monster's mouth.

Once we were out of the cave, we came to a stop at the river's edge.

"How are we going to cross it?"

My gaze dropped down to the water. My time freeze had stopped the river from flowing. It looked like black ice, with a few ripples over it from where the waves had frozen on the spot. Maybe it was actually frozen. Maybe it was solid enough that we could walk over it.

I took my spear and poked at it. The tip didn't hit something solid, not entirely anyway. It was like stabbing Jell-O. When I pulled the spear back, the tip was coated in a thick gelatinous material. It was the water, but it was congealed because it couldn't flow.

"Let's try and walk across it."

Cassandra gaped at me. "Are you sure that's a good idea?"

"No, but we have to try something. Time isn't going to stay still for long."

Lowering the spear into the river again, I used it as a stabilizer, and jumped down. My shoes immediately started to sink into the gelatinous material. We had to move quickly across, or we'd most definitely sink into it and get stuck. I wondered if this was truly the day that learning about quicksand and how to get out of it in all those cartoons was going to come in handy.

"Run across!" I said to Cassandra, so she didn't get stuck like I was about to be.

She jumped down and sprinted over the immovable river in twenty steps. I, on the other hand, was having difficulty taking my next step. I pulled the spear out and used it as a pole vaulter's pole to unstick me. Then I was able to make my next step a bit quicker, then the

next, until I fully made it to the other side and
Cassandra was pulling me up to the shoreline.

Safely across, I bent over and took in some deep
breaths to calm my racing heart. That was when I
noticed the jelly substance on the end of the spear
melted and sploshed onto the ground. Shit. Time had
started again. The rush of the river roared over us.

"Shit! Time to go!"

I took off like it was the 100-yard dash and I was in
the Olympics. Thankfully, Cassandra kept up, and we
sprinted across the field to the stone staircase as fast as
humanly possible. A distant howl echoed but I didn't
look back. Although, I did nearly throw up when I
heard a shriek and the faint thwap of wings flapping
hard.

When we reached the bottom stair of the winding
staircase, I looked all the way up and wondered how we
were going to be able to reach the top before the Furies
and Cerberus reached us and tore us into bits and
pieces.

"Could you fly us up?" I asked Cassandra.

She shrugged. "I don't know. There might not be
enough room for the full expanse of my wings."

If there wasn't enough room for hers, there
wouldn't be enough for the Furies, and there definitely
wouldn't be enough room for Cerberus's big heads to

reach us. Still, we had to try, or risk being mauled to death.

"Do it."

As she unfolded her wings, I secured my arms around her. Taking a deep breath, she flapped them once, then twice, and we rose a little. At first the tips of her wings kept hitting the sides, but she pulled them in slightly and was able to maneuver us around the stone steps, spiraling upwards, and gaining speed with every turn.

We were doing it. I nearly laughed as adrenaline shot through me. However, then I heard another war cry shriek, it was much closer, and I saw a shape moving in the shadows toward the bottom of the stairs. The Furies were fast approaching. I needed to do something.

Switching my arm around Cassandra, I was able to hold on and form a ball of fire in my hand. I made a big one, the size of a bowling ball, and tossed it down the stairs. The pain-filled screech that followed was my reward. I made another and tossed it down, then another, continuing my defense without respite—each of them bigger than the last.

By the time we reached the top, the staircase had filled with so much smoke and the stench of burning flesh and hair, that I thought we were going to choke on it. Setting me down, Cassandra kicked open the door. We tumbled out onto the grass, near the gazebo in the maze. She slammed shut the door as I snuffed out the flames in the cauldrons, effectively closing the door to anyone.

Exhausted, I fell onto my butt in the grass. Cassandra was bent over getting her wind, her hand braced against the gazebo. We both were quite aware of how close we came to dying. Then something horrible hit me.

"Holy shit. We left Tinker."

CHAPTER EIGHTEEN

NICOLE

I couldn't shake the horrible feeling I had for leaving Tinker in the Underworld with Charon. Cassandra tried to cheer me up as we made our way over the grounds and back to the academy.

"Maybe he'll enjoy the adventure."

"Charon dressed him up as a waitress and had him serving drinks. I'm not sure how much of an adventure that will be."

"He'll be okay."

"I'm just worried he'll be upset that I left him."

She gave me a look. "He's a robot. Does he even have feelings?"

"I think he does. Cade and I didn't program them into him, but I think his systems have been learning how to emote them."

"Wow."

"I know."

"Well, let's figure out if Cade is in trouble first, then we'll find a way to go and rescue Tinker." She patted my back for comfort.

Without wasting any time, we made our way over to Prometheus's Hall to talk to him. I needed to know where Cade was, and if he had any updates on their mission in Pecunia. The guards let us pass, but when Cassandra flew us up to his platform office, the big guy wasn't there.

"Do you want to go looking for him?" Cassandra asked.

"He could be anywhere." Sighing, I sat behind his desk.

Worry entered Cassandra's gaze, like I was going to get caught snooping around Prometheus's things. I didn't really care if that happened. I was sitting in his chair. So what? What was he going to do? Erase my memories and abandon me on the streets? The worst had already happened to me.

"How is he communicating with Lucian and the others while in the other realm? I know cell phones don't work. Carrier pigeons would take too long, and you'd have to train them to actually go through the portals." I was kidding with that last one, but sometimes in this place nothing surprised me.

Eyes narrowed, she stepped in closer to Prometheus's desk and picked up the square, brass lantern that had been sitting on the edge. "Lucian told me about these lanterns."

I leaned in closer as she offered it to me, and I took it. "How does it work?"

"I don't know, actually."

I looked through one of the glass panes, into the workings of it. The wick that I assumed one would need to light was visible, but after that, I couldn't understand how the communication would come through it. One of the panels was blacked out though.

"Do you think Hephaistos made it?"

She nodded. "Probably."

Still carrying it, I stood up from the desk and walked to the edge of the platform. "Then, let's go talk to Hephaistos."

When we entered his forge, the fires were flaring hot. He must've been working some metal on the top platform. Without considering whether we were interrupting him or not, we charged up the stone steps. My feet came to an abrupt stop, when I reached the top step saw twenty new eager faces turn toward me.

Whoops. I hadn't even considered that he would be holding a class, teaching new recruits. It was still strange to me that the academy got new recruits every year. However, I guessed the recruitment process didn't just stop with my year or with Cassandra's.

"Here is a prime example of things that annoy me." Hephaistos pushed up his goggles and pointed his mallet at us. "Go away."

"We really need to talk to you." I held up the lantern.

"Go away or I'll turn you into newts."

Laughter burst out of me, and I turned to the new recruits. "He's kidding. He really can't do that."

Hephaistos's glare turned nasty. "Do you want to bet on that?"

I didn't, but that still didn't mean I was going to go away.

Staring at him with a hip cocked and an eyebrow arched, I just remained there. Eventually, he'd get annoyed enough to relent to me.

He grunted, then set his mallet down on the anvil. "Oh, for Hades's sake." He stripped off his heavy leather gloves and handed them to one of the student recruits. "Take over."

The guy, who had green hair, gaped at him, looking like a guppy fish.

We watched Hephaistos stomp over to where we were. "Tell me what you want quickly, so you can get the heck out of my way."

I held up the lantern. "How does this work?"

His heavy brow furrowed with even more deep lines. "You light the wick, and it creates light that you can use to illuminate stuff with."

"Ha! You're hilarious, mate."

That rewarded me with a grunted smirk.

"How does it work for communicating? It's important. I had a… *dream*. Thanatos was there, and he mentioned Cade…" My mouth closed tightly; I didn't want to say anything else.

It was enough for Hephaistos to stop messing about though.

"Light the wick, then spin it. You're using the flames to scry through."

Cassandra nodded. "Oh, I've heard of scrying through water, using like a basin as a conduit, but I didn't know you could through fire."

"I devised the lantern to use it in the same way. To contain the power and control it. As the flames flicker, an image will broadcast against the blackened panel.

You will be able to see the other person and hear them."

After setting the lantern down onto a table, I opened one glass side and lit the wick with a flick of my finger. I grabbed the top and twisted it to get the wick inside to spin. It started slowly, then picked up speed. Every time it made a complete rotation, light flickered on the black panel.

Leaning down, so I was at eye level with it, I opened the little glass door again to speak into the lantern. "Cade?" There was no response. I tried once more. "Cade? Can you hear me? It's Nicole." Pulse racing with dread, I glanced up at Hephaistos. "This isn't working."

"Nicole?" It was faint but it was definitely Cade's voice.

My eyes snapped back to the lantern, and I looked at the black background. Squinting, I could make out a shape. I unfocused my eyes a little, and then his image became clearer. It was Cade, and he was smiling.

"Cade?"

"Yes, it's me."

"This is so weird."

"Agreed."

I laughed. "Are you okay? I had a bad dream and—"

"I was shot."

My heart lodged in my throat. "Wait, what? Did you say you were shot? Like with a gun?"

"Yeah. But I'm okay. Georgina healed me. She's amazing." He looked pained despite telling me he was okay. "But it's a lot more serious here than we first thought. There is a group mobilizing, and they are definitely dangerous."

When I glanced at Cassandra, I found the same worry in her that I was feeling. "Why don't you all return to the academy?"

"We can't. We need to find out more. I was able to talk to one of the members of this group and they are definitely recruiting and building some kind of army."

"Why? For what purpose?"

"Not quite sure yet, but there is definitely some anger at the academy and the Gods." His brow furrowed. "I thought you would have heard all of this by now. Isn't Prometheus keeping you in the loop?"

"No. This is the first time we're talking to you guys."

"You haven't seen Lucian then yet?"

"Lucian's back?" Cassandra instantly questioned, leaning down to look into the lamp.

Cade nodded. "Yes, he should have been. He left the apartment hours ago. He was returning to the academy to talk to Prometheus, and maybe bring more of you back with him."

"We haven't seen him, Cade," I confessed, because I could see the panic starting to rise in Cassandra's eyes. "Was he coming back through one of the portals?"

"Yeah, the one through the cave, like usual."

"Could he have stopped somewhere else first?"

"Not that I'm aware of." Cade shook his head. "Nic, you need to go see if he's returned. Because if he didn't get there, then something happened on this end…"

Shit. I nodded. "Yup, we'll go looking. I'll call you back in an hour."

"Okay." Licking his lips, he leaned in closer to the flames. "I love you."

Strong emotions tried to bubble up in me, but I swallowed them. "I love you, too. Talk soon, yeah?"

Nodding, his image vanished as he blew out his flame. My hand landed on the lantern to stop the wick from spinning, and I straightened, glancing over at Cassandra. Her face was paler than usual, so I grabbed her hand.

"We'll go look for him. That was probably why Prometheus wasn't in his office. He was meeting with Lucian somewhere on the grounds to talk about what's going on."

"Yes." She cleared her throat. "That must be it."

"We'll search every inch of this place, and then go to the portal in the cave and wait." I squeezed her hand. "Okay, mate?"

"Okay."

I picked up the lantern, I definitely wasn't leaving it here, then gave Hephaistos a nod. "Thanks for—"

"Yup." His gaze flitted over Cassandra then back to me. "Make sure to keep me updated. I want to know what's going on."

"I will."

After leaving the forge, we searched the entire academy. We went from one hall to another, and talked to everyone we knew, recruits, Demigods, and Gods alike. No one had seen Lucian since leaving a day ago.

We checked every training field, every dorm room, the maze, and even the stables. Again, no one had seen him. Prometheus was also missing in action, and it wasn't like he was an easy person to miss.

At the end, we decided to go to the cave and check on the portal to the mortal realm. Sometimes portals could be shut down. Maybe that was why Lucian hadn't arrived yet. It had happened before, but it could only be done from inside the academy.

I stood with Cassandra on the edge of the pool, glancing down into the clear, dark blue water. So far, there wasn't any indication that anyone had come through it. There was no water up on the rocks, where a person would've had to pull themselves out of it.

"I'm sure he's okay," I assured her. "Lucian is like the toughest bloke I know. He has more power in his pinky finger than all of us put together." Fine, so I didn't know if that was true, but it sounded like it could be. Lucian was pretty bad ass.

She nodded, but continued wringing her hands together with worry.

I was about to suggest that we maybe dive in and go check the portal ourselves, when ripples surged through the pool. Someone was coming up for air.

"There he is." I patted her shoulder. "We were all worried for nothing."

The ripples got bigger and bigger, until a head broke through the surface. Except, it wasn't a blond head, it was a large one with brown curly hair. Prometheus swam to the edge of the pool and pulled himself out of the water.

The moment he stood, steam rose off his skin and clothes—he'd dried himself off internally. His eyes bounced from me to Cassandra. "What are you two doing here?"

"We heard Lucian was supposed to be returning to

the academy hours ago," I explained. "We looked everywhere for him but couldn't find him."

The headmaster shook his head. "He won't be able to return. The portal's been closed. No one can get through it."

CHAPTER NINETEEN

CADE

*a*fter I blew out the lantern's flame, I called Jasmine and Georgina into the room. The others were out doing more recon and intel gathering.

"What's up?" Jasmine's face pinched in concern.

"I don't think Lucian made it back to the academy."

"What? How do you know?" Georgina sunk into the chair beside the bed.

"I just talked to Nicole." I pointed to the lantern. "They haven't seen him. She was with Cassandra, and she hasn't seen him either."

"Could just mean he went to see Prometheus immediately upon returning…"

"He left hours ago." I sighed. "It takes, what? Fifteen minutes to fly to Kios, another ten to swim through the portal. He may have gone to see Prometheus first, but there's no way he didn't check in with Cassandra. Besides that, I asked him to check in on Nicole for me. I had a bad feeling that something had happened to her. He said he would, and I know he would have."

Jasmine began to pace in front of the bed. "Shit. Are you suggesting that he's been… taken, or hurt?"

"I think we have to consider that is a possibility and prepare to defend ourselves."

"Do you really think it will come to that?"

"They shot me. I have no doubt in my mind that if they could've killed me, they would have. I'm certain that they shot Tom to silence him. These people are dangerous. They mean to start a war." I swung my legs over the side of the bed, grimacing as I did.

Georgina tried to push me back into the mattress. "You still need healing."

"I don't think I have the luxury of that anymore. We need to get the others and forge a plan."

"Should we all go back to the academy?" Jasmine asked.

Pausing, I thought about that for a minute. It would definitely be the safest place for us, but then we'd be abandoning the people of Pecunia, and of the other Greek cities that were seeing vandalism on their temples and civil disorder. If we fled, then who would stand up to defend them?

I shook my head. "No, I think we should stay and figure out how to defeat this group. We aren't the only people in harm's way. Yesterday's paint ball incident was just a test. A warning."

"These people can't possibly think that they are going to win against the Gods."

The words Prometheus had said earlier echoed in my head, about the strength in numbers, the power in numbers. There was way more of them than there was of us right now. Even though we had Godly powers that they couldn't even imagine, they had guns, machines, and a common enemy. There would be no winner in this battle.

"Maybe it's not about winning," I considered.

"Revenge?"

"I think it's about justice. There is real emotional pain behind this." Tom's face popped into my mind, the emotion in his eyes when he spoke was real. That was a parent's pain. He was speaking to me as a father who would do anything for his children.

"You think it all started by one person?" Jasmine frowned.

"Aren't all movements started from one small point?" We needed to find out who was at the center of this whole thing. My thoughts kept returning to the man named Mark. Maybe he was the single fuse that had been lit.

"I'll text the others to get back to the apartment." Jasmine took out the burner phone from her pocket and started sending those texts.

As she did that, I got to my feet under Georgina's watchful eye. The simple movement made me sweat, and she gave me a knowing look. One that told me she'd take no issue with pushing me back into the bed and knocking me out with one of Chiron's special brews.

"Just give me something to help, Gina. Because I'm not sitting on my ass."

Resigned, she went into her leather pouch and took out a plastic sandwich baggy. Inside were what looked like a bunch of peanut butter balls. Something you might get in a trendy, health food store. She took one out and handed it to me.

"Eat it. It's something I concocted to give you extra energy and strength."

"Do I even want to know what's in it?"

"Nope."

I trusted her, so I popped it into my mouth and chewed. It tasted earthy, but nothing too gag-inducing. Swallowing it, I took a hearty drink of water. "Thanks."

In the middle of a text, Jasmine's phone rang. "Hello?" She listened for a moment. "Hang back, don't bring attention to yourself, okay? We're coming." Ending the call, she turned to us, worry furrowing her brow. "That was Mia. She said there is a mob forming in the square. They have quite a few people and a bullhorn. They are saying the Demigods are dangerous, that we aren't here to protect them but to oppress them, and they are calling for Melany's statue to be pulled down."

"Holy crap." Georgina sunk down in the chair.

Pacing once more, her go-to way of dealing with stress, Jasmine nodded. "Yeah, it's bad."

"Okay, let's get prepared for anything, and go to the square."

"What if they discover who we are and turn on us?" Georgina's face paled.

"I'm going there to reveal myself," I informed, knowing it sounded insane.

"What the hell are you suggesting?" Jasmine asked.

Jasmine was going to be the one who I would need

to convince. Out of everyone here, she was the most like Lucian. A soldier, a warrior. Ready to fight. However, right now we needed a tactician, a negotiator, if we were going to stop this before it got really out of hand.

"I'm going to talk to the people. All they are getting is a bunch of brainwashing bullshit. They have to be reminded of all the good we've done for the town, for the country, and for the world."

"What if they shoot you again?" Georgina lifted her eyebrows.

"They aren't going to shoot me in front of everyone. I was unlucky before, letting them sneak up on me away from curious eyes. That was my mistake. One I won't make again."

Jasmine didn't look convinced. "I don't think it's a good idea, but I'm not going to talk you out of it."

"I won't out any of you. You stay on the outskirts, be alert and prepared in case it all turns to shit. If it does, defend yourselves, and if it really goes sideways, get to a portal and get back to the academy."

"Okay." Jasmine went into the other room to, I assumed, arm herself and get prepared.

"Do you need any help?" Georgina asked, but I shook my head.

"Make sure everyone keeps a level head. The last

thing we need is a bunch of civil casualties. That will not help our cause, just theirs."

Standing, she patted me on the shoulder. "We're lucky that you're here." With a tight smile, she walked out of the room.

Before I followed them out, I opened the lantern and lit the wick. I needed to talk to Nicole, because I was about to do something reckless and foolish, which would possibly get me even more hurt than I was.

When the flame sparked, I sent it spinning.

"Nicole?" I hoped she had the lantern with her and was in a situation where she could talk to me. "Can you hear me? It's Cade."

A few minutes went by, and I was about to give up, when I heard her voice.

"I'm here."

I squinted at the black panel on the side of the lantern and saw her highlighted face. Relief flowed through me, and I relaxed a little. "I haven't got long to talk. Things have escalated—"

"Lucian isn't here. He never showed."

"I know." I nodded. "We think he may have been taken by the anti-God group."

"Bloody hell. What should we do?"

"There's a mob forming here, at Melany's statue. I'm going to go talk to them and—"

"You are going to what?!"

"Listen, it will be okay. People are just confused and angry. They want to know that it's okay."

"Cade, don't you dare do something stupid!"

"I won't. I promise. But what I need you to do is to find out some information. I'm pretty sure that the leader of all of this is a parent of someone who either went to the academy or didn't get an invite. His first name is Mark. That's all I've got but maybe you can find a way to do something with that."

"I'll see what I can do."

"Good."

"I don't like that you're talking to me like you're not going to see me again."

I chuckled to ease the tension, but I knew she'd see past it. It was true, I was scared that I wouldn't see her after this. "You'll see me again, Nic. After I talk everyone down, I'll get to the portal—"

"The portals are not—"

The flame in the lantern blew out, and with it, so did the image of Nicole and her voice.

Reaching in I tried to relight it, but for some reason that I couldn't discern, it wouldn't ignite.

A sense of dread washed over me.

Georgina stood in the bedroom doorway. "You ready to go?"

I gave the lantern one last look, then nodded. Rolling my shoulders, I started for the door, and with each step I took I felt better and better. The energy ball Georgina gave me must have kicked into effect. When I reached the doorway and stepped out into the living room, I didn't even feel the bullet wound anymore. There was still a tightness there, like my skin was being pulled, but I didn't have any pain.

It must've shown on my face because Georgina gave me a knowing smile. "Feeling better?"

"Oh, yeah. Much better." A surge of adrenaline coursed through me, and I rolled my shoulders again. It felt like I could run a marathon or lift five hundred pounds without breaking a sweat. "You're a genius, Gina."

Her cheeks blushed a little at the compliment.

Jasmine smacked her on the back. "She is a genius."

We left the apartment and made our way to the town square. The sounds coming from the commotion reached us before we saw it, whoever was speaking was using a bullhorn to deliver his rhetoric. There were some enthusiastic responses from the crowd, but I figured those people were already part of the group, and were planted there to gain support. It was a trick I'd seen used many times.

There had to have been about a hundred people milling about the square and the monument. For the most part, it appeared that the majority were just there out of curiosity. There were a few loud voices in the multitude, but not enough to convince me that the guy with the loud voice was making any headway with the citizens of Pecunia.

Mia and Diego met us as we approached the edge of the gathering. Jasmine and Mia hugged.

"Where are the others?" I asked.

"Jia and Marek are on the other side. Rosie and Ren are somewhere in the middle, I believe, closest to Melany's statue." Diego gestured to the murmuring crowd. "Charlotte and Ezra are at the far end, closer to the temple. What's the play here?"

"I'm going to address the crowd as someone from the academy."

Diego's expression grew serious. "Are you sure that's wise?"

"I don't know, but we can't let this group's message grow. Without a response, it will become insidious." I checked myself to make sure I wasn't bleeding. "If you sense it's getting out of hand, then get out of here. Meet in Kios, at the portal."

Grabbing her phone, Jasmine texted that info to the others.

With one last nod to them, I made my way through the multitude toward the front, next to the guy with the bullhorn. As I got closer, I eyed him, but he didn't look familiar. I was sure he wasn't one of the men who had shot at me. However, I did recognize another man standing nearby. He'd been in the SUV. He wasn't the one with the gun though.

I climbed onto a big rock that was in the square. It had rope around it and a sign that said, "Do Not Climb," but I didn't think anyone was going to give me a ticket over it.

"Hello!" I waved at the crowd, interrupting the guy with the bullhorn mid-speech. "Hello. My name is Cade, and I'm from the academy."

That caused a stir through the crowd. The guy I recognized pointed at me. "He's one of them! He's a freak!"

"I am one of 'them', but I am not a freak." I even did air quotes. "I was invited to the academy when I turned eighteen, and went to train there to be a soldier—"

"To kill us!" the guy with the bullhorn shouted.

"That's a lie," I stated. "We train there to protect YOU." I waved a hand over the crowd. "All of you. Just like Melany did, in the great battle with the Titans." I gestured to her statue. "She, and the others like her, fought to save this town from destruction, fought to save you from—"

"He killed Tom!" the man in the crowd shouted, pointing an accusatory finger at me.

Shit. I hadn't expected that.

Several faces frowned at me, and there was a concerned murmur through the multitude.

I put my hands out toward the people. "I did not KILL anyone. In fact, these men tried to kill me." I lifted my shirt to reveal the bandage around my waist. "They shot me."

"Liar!" the bullhorn guy shouted, nearly busting out everyone's ear drums. "We have video proof! We have video of this one flying Tom out of the temple and taking him to a field outside of town and killing him!"

This was not going well.

Glancing across the gathering of people, I met Jasmine's gaze and shook my head, hoping that she got the message… to get the hell out of there.

"Go to our website nomoregods.com and see for yourself!"

Everyone in front of me started to murmur concerns and questions to each other. None of them sounded hopeful. It was time for us to leave before it got out of hand. An angry mob was dangerous, even to a Demigod.

My wings unfurled, which drew some surprised gasps from people in the crowd. When I took to the sky, shouts followed.

"Get him!"

"Don't let him get away!"

As I got higher, I saw the others also take to the sky. More shouts came from the people. The next moment, two men in black shot something into the air, toward Rosie and Ren, who were trying desperately to get away. It unraveled in the sky, revealing it was a net. Yet, it was like no net I'd ever seen. It covered Rosie, crushing her wings, and she dropped to the ground.

My heart sank into my gut.

We were not going to get out of here without a fight.

Extending my arms out to my sides, held my hands open wide as fire ignited along my fingers.

CHAPTER TWENTY

NICOLE

I shook the lantern, hoping to make it work again, but I knew I was being foolish. I was just doing it out of frustration. After the flame blew out and I lost contact with Cade, it felt like my heart was going to implode.

Once Prometheus found out the portal to Kios had been shut down, he had Cassandra and I, as well as others he recruited, check out all the remaining portals to the mortal realm...

They had all been shut.

No one could get to the academy or the grounds surrounding it, and no one could get out.

Not through conventional means, anyway. I didn't know if the Gods had other secret ways, I was sure they did, but they weren't sharing that knowledge with us.

Going to the training field near the time garden, I checked on the portal I used to come from Paris, and discovered it, too, was shut down. It had to have been done from inside the academy, as I didn't think anyone in the mortal realms had that kind of power. Were the angry people rising up against us, being helped by one of us? To me, that would've been contradictory, but I'd seen people do odd things and make bad decisions against their own morals and rationale.

Confused and worried, I returned to the garden and sat on the bench, our bench, the one Cade and I had sat on so many times before, with a sigh. I needed a moment to think. Everything was happening too fast, and I didn't know what to do. Cade and the others were obviously in trouble, but there wasn't anything I could do from here, since the portals were shut.

Cade had mentioned doing some research to find out who was behind all of this. I could do that, at least. All I had was a first name, Mark, but I could work with it. I just needed access to information that I wasn't sure the academy was going to appreciate me snooping through.

I thought about doing a time jump. Maybe I could

go back to yesterday, in Pecunia, and pre-empt all of this, but what if I made a mistake and made it worse? Playing around in the past was not a good idea. I was starting to understand that.

Still, I had to try something.

Concentrating on Melany's statue in the city, I thought about the day, when I was there with Cade. My mind focused on the color of the stone, and Melany's fierce face carved into it. I closed my eyes and thought about the town square—the lush green grass, and big fig trees, the smell of the flowers growing in a planter nearby.

The air started to vibrate against my skin, and I knew it was shimmering around me. Every inch of me tensed, getting ready to be sucked into the white void of time and space, hoping beyond hope that I ended up where I wanted to go, and at the right time.

As I was being pulled out of the present, flashes of Melany sped by in my mind, on a loop. It made me dizzy, making my stomach roll over like ocean waves. Then everything came to a sudden halt, and I tumbled onto the ground.

Except, it wasn't the green grass of the town square I had been expecting but pure darkness.

I reached out a hand to feel the "floor". It was definitely solid, so I didn't have a fear of falling into some inescapable black hole of eternal existence. That would've sucked. However, this definitely was not the void I usually came into when time jumping. This was different. It almost felt like the dark cave from Cassandra's vision, when we moved through dimensions.

Creating a ball of fire, I stood, spinning around in every direction to try to orient myself. It was pitch black all around me, so I guessed I should just start walking. I picked a spot to my right, and moved that way, careful with every step, just in case I did fall off the edge of the world.

After a few more steps, I got the sense I was emerging into a room. There was a faint glow ahead of me. Not of direct light exactly, but of substance. My eyes started to make out furniture—the outline of a four-poster bed, and a side night table. Whose room had I popped into?

Before I could even make a guess, I was grabbed by the front of my shirt, and slammed against a wall.

"Who the hell are you?" someone hissed into my face, pressing the tip of a sharp blade against my throat.

Narrowing my eyes, I made out their face—sharp features, strong chin, fierce eyes, a lightning scar along one cheek, blue hair fluttering along arched eyebrows.

"Melany?"

She frowned, and slowly, the knife lowered from my neck. I suspected a bead of my blood was left on the tip.

Melany finally stepped back, taking a good look at me. "I know you, right?"

"Yeah, sort of." I cleared my throat, trying to regain my composure. "I'm Nicole. We've talked a couple of times."

Confused, she backed up even further and sat on the edge of the big bed. I must've woken her.

While she processed that, I took that moment to look around the space. We were definitely in a bedroom, and it seemed eerily similar to the one I'd slept in at Hade's Hall. Same type of furniture, same dark, rich color scheme. Where the hell were we? Had I stepped into the afterlife? Or, I supposed, Melany's version of the afterlife?

"I've had dreams about you." She lifted her head and eyed me warily. "And I remember the two times seeing you through…"

"A portal."

"Yeah, that. What's going on?"

It felt a bit awkward to just stand there in front of her, so I sat in the velvety chair next to a vanity table, though its presence there was weird. Melany didn't seem like a girl to primp and pamper herself, or spend hours on her makeup. I was pretty sure she didn't even wear it.

"I'm not entirely sure, to be honest. I don't know why I keep opening portals to… ah, you. But I suspect it's for a reason."

Her gaze narrowed. "You can open portals? Like to other places?"

"They are usually time portals. Like, I can jump through time. Except, I don't think what brought me to you was a jump through time, exactly."

"You asked me before *where* I was. What did you mean by that?"

"Um…" I didn't know how to answer that. I wasn't sure if she knew what happened to her. Or I could be very wrong, and she was completely and utterly aware to the point of pain.

She gestured to the room where we were. "I'm here, in this room, in Hade's Hall, with Hades."

"Well," I grimaced. "You're not actually in Hade's Hall."

She made a face, like I was an idiot. "Riiight. Of course, I am."

"Melany, you do know you are dead, right?"

Laughter burst out of her. "Okay." She shook her head. "Did Hades put you up to this? Cuz it's not really funny." Getting to her feet, she turned toward the bedroom door. "Hades! This isn't funny, Babe."

"Do you remember the academy?"

Her attention returned to me. "Yeah. What about it?"

"And Lucian, Jasmine, and Georgina?"

Her brow furrowed. "Of course, I remember my friends."

"Do you remember what happened to you?"

She opened her mouth like she was going to respond, but then snapped it shut, sinking back onto the bed. Her finger slid down her cheek, dragging over her scars. I didn't know if it was a conscious thing or if she did it reflexively.

"Who are you again?"

"I'm Nicole."

"Are you a Goddess?"

I snorted. "Shit no, mate. I'm just a girl who went to the academy, just like you did. And a bunch of bad stuff happened to me, just like to you."

"You said you know Lucian?"

"I do. He's a decent bloke. Has bit of a stick up his ass, but other than that, I like him just fine."

She chuckled at that. "I think I miss him."

"Well, he misses you. They all do. All your friends

back at the academy. I think even Hephaistos misses you. Although he won't admit it, he's such a grump."

Melany's hand lifted to her forehead, and she began to rub it incessantly back and forth. Like she was trying to scrub away the cobwebs that covered her mind. "I'm having trouble understanding what's going on right now."

My chest tightened, and I got up from the chair, sitting beside her on the bed. "Hey, me too, mate. I never know what the hell is going on. I usually just go with the flow."

Her gaze fixed on me, and it was intense. "Has something happened to Lucian and my friends?"

"Yeah. They're in trouble, and I think I'm here because you might be the only one who can save them."

"I'm stuck here, I think." She frowned. "Although, I know I chose to be here. With Hades."

"It's okay that you chose to be here, Melany. No one's judging you. I'm not. Hades is fine as hell."

She laughed again. "You've met him?"

"A couple of times. A long, long time ago though. Like three thousand years, give or take." Confusion captured her expression once more, but I shrugged. "Don't worry about it. It's hard to explain."

Shit, all of this was difficult to explain. Even to myself.

"So, what do you think about coming back to the academy with me?"

Her head twitched, and she licked her lips. It looked like she was having some kind of reaction to my question. Maybe whatever had brought her here, wanted to keep her here. Whether that was an actual entity, or her own physiology. If she was truly dead, then maybe Thanatos couldn't allow her to leave.

Screw Death. I wanted to give it a go anyway.

"Can I come back?" Her voice was small. It was the first time I'd heard her sound afraid or unsure. Two things I thought I'd never see from the fierce warrior everyone talked about with awe and reverence.

Determination rushed through me, and I got to my feet, holding out my hand to her. "I don't know. But let's try it, eh?"

She hesitated.

"Only if you want to, though. I won't force you to do something you don't want to do. I'm one hundred percent about free will, mate."

After another few moments, ones where I could see she was struggling, she placed her hand in mine and stood. "Sure. Why not? I haven't been on an adventure in a while."

I smiled at her, loving her bravado.

"All right. Hold on to me. It might be a really bumpy ride."

I pictured the academy, the time garden specifically. My mind filled with it, and I held on to the image tightly, keeping it solid and at the forefront. All the smells and feelings I'd experienced when I was sitting near the sundial awoke, swirling around me. I saw Cade's face smiling at me.

The air began to thin and quiver. Little hairs on my arms rose to attention, and a feeling of vertigo settled inside my stomach, like I was lurching to the side. Then we were sucked into the void. It was black, as before, and that made me start to panic. What if I wasn't taking us back to the academy but somewhere else, to another dimension? One we would never be able to escape?

It felt like our bodies tumbled over and over, doing somersaults in mid-air, and I suddenly lost Melany's hand. I couldn't feel it in mine. Oh, Gods, what if I'd sent her spiralling into nothingness?

What if I condemned her to a place and time that didn't exist? Where Melany would stop existing?

My form crashed onto a spot of soft grass near the sundial. I felt sick. I'd messed around with something that I didn't have any business getting into, losing

Melany because of it. I was never going to be able to forgive myself.

A loud gasp broke my thoughts, and I turned my head to see Cassandra standing there, her face paler than normal. Her hand flew to her mouth as she looked at something past me.

"Oh, my Gods! I can't believe it."

Scrambling to my feet, I swiveled around, shock and relief running through me.

There was she, standing with both hands on her hips, a bit of a scowl to her mouth.

I'd done the unthinkable.

I'd brought Melany home.

Thanks for reading *Darkness Rising*. Don't miss all the new adventures in Demigods Academy 11! And if you loved this book, consider leaving a review on Amazon.

Just one or two lines would be very helpful to

support us.

Hugs,

Elisa & Kiera

ABOUT THE AUTHORS

Elisa S. Amore is the number-one bestselling author of the paranormal romance saga *Touched*.

Vanity Fair Italy called her "the undisputed queen of romantic fantasy." After the success of Touched, she produced the audio version of the saga featuring Hollywood star Matt Lanter (*90210, Timeless, Star Wars*) and Disney actress Emma Galvin, narrator of *Twilight* and *Divergent*. Elisa is now a full-time writer of young adult fantasy. She's wild about pizza and also loves traveling, which she calls a source of constant inspiration. With her successful series about life and death, Heaven and Hell, she has built a loyal fanbase on social media that continues to grow, and has quickly become a favorite author for thousands of readers in the U.S.

Visit Elisa S. Amore's website and join her List of Readers at www.ElisaSAmore.com and Text AMORE to (844) 339 0303 for new release alerts.

FOLLOW ELISA S. AMORE:
facebook.com/eli.amore

instagram.com/eli.amore
twitter.com/ElisaSAmore
tiktok.com/@ElisaSAmore
facebook.com/groups/amoreans
elisa.amore@touchedsaga.com

***

Kiera Legend writes Urban Fantasy and Paranormal Romance stories that bite. She loves books, movies and Tv-Shows. Her best friends are usually vampires, witches, werewolves and angels. She never hangs out without her little dragon. She especially likes writing kick-ass heroines and strong world-buildings and is excited for all the books that are coming!

Text LEGEND to (844) 339 0303 to don't miss any of them (US only) or sign up at www.kieralegend.com to get an email alert when her next book is out.

FOLLOW KIERA LEGEND:
facebook.com/groups/kieralegend
facebook.com/kieralegend
authorkieralegend@gmail.com